W9-BRM-310

OTHER PEOPLE'S
LOVE AFFAIRS

Other People's Love Affairs

⟨⟩

STORIES

D. WYSTAN OWEN

ALGONQUIN BOOKS

OF CHAPEL HILL 2018

Published by
Algonquin Books of Chapel Hill
Post Office Box 2225
Chapel Hill, North Carolina 27515-2225

a division of
Workman Publishing
225 Varick Street
New York, New York 10014

© 2018 by D. Wystan Owen.
All rights reserved.
Printed in the United States of America.
Published simultaneously in Canada by Thomas Allen & Son Limited.
Design by Steve Godwin.

"What Is Meant to Remain" appeared in *A Public Space* no. 11 (2010) as
"The Dentist's Chair"; "Housekeeper" appeared in *The Threepenny Review* no. 124
(Winter 2011); "Other People's Love Affairs" appeared in
The American Scholar (Summer 2012).

This is a work of fiction. While, as in all fiction, the literary perceptions and insights
are based on experience, all names, characters, places, and incidents either are products
of the author's imagination or are used fictitiously.

LIBRARY OF CONGRESS CATALOGING-IN-PUBLICATION DATA
Library of Congress Cataloging-in-Publication Data
Names: Owen, D. Wystan, author.
Title: Other people's love affairs : stories / D. Wystan Owen.
Description: First edition. | Chapel Hill, North Carolina : Algonquin Books
of Chapel Hill, 2018.
Identifiers: LCCN 2018011884 | ISBN 9781616207052 (trade pbk. original : alk. paper)
Subjects: LCSH: Small cities—England—Fiction. | Man-woman
relationships—Fiction. | England—Social life and customs—Fiction. |
LCGFT: Psychological fiction. | Short stories.
Classification: LCC PS3615.W35 A6 2018 | DDC 813.6—dc23
LC record available at https://lccn.loc.gov/2018011884

10 9 8 7 6 5 4 3 2 1
First Edition

For my mother, Julie;
for my father, Geoffrey.

And, always, for Ellen Kamoe.

CONTENTS

X X X

OTHER PEOPLE'S
LOVE AFFAIRS

Ж

Lovers of a Kind

✕ ✕ ✕

In Glass, along the boardwalk overlooking the sea, near the old village shops or the park's promenades, where in winter great bulbs will be hung from tree boughs and snow fine as dust will settle beneath them, Wen Whitaker can be seen of a morning, collecting rubbish to put in his pram. His figure, when one comes upon him, is stooped, his head moving gently as if in suspension. It does not cause alarm, the frank vagrancy of him. He is known and remembered; he has always been here.

His hair is stark white, a blown bit of cotton; the backs of his hands are like dark, weathered wood. Some speculate that Wen is a gypsy, others that his father was a sailor from Crete. For his own part, he is unconcerned with such questions, content so long as he isn't harassed. He wants only to gather his rubbish, observe the movement of other lives by the sea. In times past he had further desires, but those days of wanting are many years gone.

Past the gown shop he walks, past the bank, past the Green Man; he moves slowly where the surface is cobbled, pauses sometimes at the post office window to admire new editions of stamps on display. Everywhere he is pushing his pram. Locals ask him what is on at the Gem, knowing he will have taken note in his rounds.

His home is a small hut near the sea, where the beaches and cliffs lining most of the shore give way to salt marsh, then woods of live oak. Made of stone, it was built as a fisherman's shelter. He knows that he is assumed to be homeless but is proud of this building in which he was born. On the mantel over the disused coke stove, he keeps the treasures he has found through the years: a brass fishing lure, a length of white ribbon, a cigarette lighter engraved TLG. On the floor is a mattress with sheets he tucks up, two blankets for when the evening is cold. With his government check he keeps the water and light on. He sells his rubbish by the pound to the city.

Saturdays he takes a meal at St. Simon, Sundays at Temple Beth Elohim. Hot dinners there, soup or spaghetti, sometimes cocoa or tea at the end. Wednesdays at the hospital a meal is provided also, a small tray brought to the courtyard for him.

From a window overlooking the hospital grounds, Eleanor Cartwright watches him eat. He sits on a bench with his back to the wall, hunched over, trying not to disturb. Always, he begins with his pot of ice cream, anxious in case such a rare thing should melt. He thanks her when she hands him his meal, but there is a distant formality to it: he doesn't smile, their eyes seldom meet. It saddens her, that, for they used to be friends. Briefly they were. Lovers of a kind. The sort of thing you only recognized after. That has been the way of love in her life: a feeling understood only after it leaves, discernible in the hollow space of its absence, known only as a haunting, a ghost.

It began around the time her mother went missing, a disappearance not in itself out of character but that seemed in its persistence to mark the ultimate severance of a long-fraying bond with the world. Through the years, there had been occasional madness. A hospitalization when, just after Eleanor's birth, her father had opened the door to the bathroom to find his wife attempting to drown their new daughter. In Eleanor's own memory there had been signs of it, too: maternal affection overwhelming, assaultive, given and withdrawn with equal caprice. She remembered her mother leaving—sometimes for days—and returning unwashed, unspeaking, exhausted. Afterward, there would be stretches of normalcy, an uneasy equilibrium struck. But lately, her father had said, the spells had grown more frequent and lasting, discrete clouds merging, blotting the sun.

"It's good of you to have visited, button." At the kitchen table he spoke. With his hands, he wiped away tears from his face.

"Oh, Daddy," Eleanor said.

She had come back to see about him, not revealing her intention to stay. She had boarded all through her grammar school years, glumly accepting the necessity of it, and now had lived for years at a distance, persisting in a spoiled affair.

The police had been alerted already. They'd stood about, not urgent in manner. A grown woman could not be compelled to come home.

"She's unwell," Mr. Cartwright had said.

"But you say she's done this before? And she's taken money and clothes?"

They would merely keep out an eye. The standard reports would be filed.

"I'll be all right, button. I will. It's all right," he assured her. "Go on with your life."

But she found she scarcely knew what that meant. She hadn't left much behind in the city—a few friends, her erstwhile lover. Cheaply, she took a small flat in Glass, on the outskirts where dwellings stood in meek rows and a B-picture house had fallen to ruin. In the damp, dingy space of her rooms, she tried to arrange the details of a life: On her desk, a book where she kept her accounts, a typewriter, a photograph of her mother taken in one happy stretch between spells. In the pantry, just enough food for the week, fruits and vegetables rationed with care. Her bed was pushed far into a corner, a sensible twin with a wrought-iron frame. And in the dresser, a small bag of grass: the remains of what had been an eighth of an ounce.

She applied to Mercy's maternity ward, having worked in reception at a clinic in town. The woman there said there wasn't a place, but she might need assistance in Specialty Care.

"Neonatal, that is," she said, lifting her eyes. Beatrice, it said on her breast.

Eleanor nodded and said that was fine.

"Reception, a few other menial things. That's if we don't have enough volunteers."

Days, she would move from one room to the next, regard infants like sea creatures washed onto shore, writhing in a vain effort to swim. Their fingers strained against something unseen; their skin was as pale and thin as wet cloth. She watched as they moved in that way, at times overwhelmed by tenderness for them: the unlikeliness, the accident of their lives.

She hadn't been loved by the man in the city, nor by the men who had come before him. Traveling to and from Mercy, she knew this. She rode a blue bike, bought secondhand. At night, fog settled onto the road. She'd been thought beautiful, that was all. Lovely, her pale eyes had often been called, her black hair, the childish turn of her mouth. Perhaps it was the dull practicality of her, the way she wasn't given to dream. In every affair she'd been trying it on, a weak effort at madness, romance. She considered this, too, riding about, how she'd only thought to run as far as the sea.

From her first days back, she would see him in town: the old vagrant picking trash from the road. Often she noticed people like him. One day he was near the marina; the next he was outside the chemist on Lynn. She didn't know why his image remained, only that it was insistently there: his curiosity when he lifted an item, his pleasure when he turned it about in his hand.

Specialty Care was a small, well-lit ward, managed by Beatrice during the day shift and visited by a number of doctors in what seemed a haphazard rotation. Only seldom were any volunteers to be found—teenagers or pairs of old ladies—and so she began to handle the infants, rocking them slowly back and forth in her arms. She did not touch those who had tubes in their bodies, fed only those deemed healthy enough. It was far more than she'd been asked to do in her previous job, but she dared not demur for need of the work.

"Only we're doing the best we know how," she would whisper, touching a minuscule hand. "Only we are making our way."

The weak bodies had a curious warmth.

Beatrice showed her how to massage them, applying pressure along the length of their arms. She was firm with them, unsentimental; she cursed when her arthritic knuckles seized up.

"You aren't going to hurt them," she said. "Trust me. They're dying to feel something, Ellie."

It was another sort of love, watching Beatrice work. The unthinking competence of her.

"Being born," she said, "is a terrible thing. Everyone living has suffered that loss."

"SHE HASN'T ACCESSED any funds from the bank," Eleanor's father said on the phone. "Though I don't think I should have expected her to."

Eleanor lay on the floor of her room, her back to the carpet, the phone to her ear. On the ceiling, a large stain resembled Japan.

"You're well then, button?"

"Oh, well enough."

"These cataracts are a nuisance."

Things sometimes were not easy between them. His had always been a kind, gentle presence, but mild almost to the point of detachment; in the reigning atmosphere of volatile passion, his steadiness had often seemed an indifference. That in adulthood she had grown to be like him only increased the resentment she held. *My darling*, the man in the city had called her. *Nothing I offered was ever enough.*

"I shall have to have the surgery, after all," her father said now. "It's awful, the thought of cutting an eye."

From above, she could hear Mrs. Ridgewe's TV, the laugh track from a comedy show. The laughter was constant, night after night, but never belonged to Mrs. Ridgewe herself. She was a middle-aged woman, well dressed in old clothes, the elaborate maquillage of her face suggesting a lifelong dissatisfaction. Her step on the landing was sharp. In the shared kitchen she ate kippers for breakfast.

At length, Eleanor rang off with her father and smoked a little bit of the grass. She liked to have a bit now and then while she tidied or reviewed lists of chores to be done. Her second neighbor was a man: Deegan Kirby. She liked him more than she did Mrs. Ridgewe. He could be seen some nights on the landing, dressed outrageously, coming or going: as a pirate, or in high heels and a gown. He ran a burlesque show on weekends in Croft; days, he kept books for a grocery chain. The first time she'd seen him dressed as a woman, she'd looked down, afraid to have caught him at something.

"Eleanor, darling. Come," he had said. "Be a dear and hold my martini a moment."

She had done so, blushing while he straightened his dress. He hadn't shaved the backs of his hands.

"That's better. These dresses will chafe you to death. I'm slimming to get myself down to a twenty."

She'd wondered later if he might be embarrassed. He had about him an air of performance, a way of too much protesting his ease. Sometimes she heard his voice through the walls, shouting hoarsely into the phone.

Another joke inspired laughter upstairs.

"Of course I want to know she's all right," her father had said as they prepared to ring off. "But I won't say there isn't relief," and though Eleanor understood what he meant, indeed had entertained the same thought herself, she'd been angry, feeling he hadn't the right.

SHE HAD OCCASION to speak to the man. It was evening, the last of the light going down.

A spring rain had halted her under a bridge, where the road ran beside a creek feeding the sea. She leaned her bike against the side of the bridge and paused to pull up the hood of her mack. On the surface of the water, ripples expanded, as if schools of fish were rising to feed. At a distance she could see him approaching, his head bobbing up and down in the rain.

As he drew near, he squinted, trying to place her. For a moment, she felt the hand of fear on her heart. He stopped then and stood before her under the bridge. He opened the canvas top of his pram.

"Clever, this," he said, gesturing to it.

She looked. Nobody else was about.

"Some things'd be all right in the rain: metal and glass. It's paper that spoils." He unfurled a banner from a juggling show. "All dry and good as new. See?" he said.

The season was changing. She didn't feel chilled, despite the deluge. Along the strand, vendors, absent all winter, had returned; only that morning she'd passed them, each staring, untrusting, up at the sky. Books, they sold; pinwheels, T-shirts, and candy.

"All right, then?" Eleanor said. "You've had a bit of a soak yourself, sir."

His white hair had become matted and wet. The wool of his coat was heavy about him.

"Right as rain." He laughed to himself. "It's *All of a Piece* at the Gem tonight, dear."

The rain, already, had slowed to a drizzle. In the silence, she was aware of her breathing.

"That's how the cinema's called. Did you know that?"

She nodded.

"Of course. My apologies, dear. Silly, thinking you'd not be aware."

"You weren't to know."

"Ah, but I was. Aren't you Eleanor Cartwright?"

He didn't look at her when he spoke. His eyes moved possessively over his rubbish. She wondered if he had been following her. Surely, she'd been the subject of talk—she was still known sometimes in shops and cafés, oblique reference made to her family crisis—but she could not imagine that sort of gossip finding its way to an old vagrant's ears.

Thunder sounded a good distance off.

"I was friends with your mother," he said.

At work, Beatrice told her his name.

"He's missing a screw, but harmless," she said.

They were crossing the hallway to Specialty Care. The sound of their heavy clogs echoed about them.

"That pram of his," Eleanor said. "I thought it might be he'd taken a child."

"Oh, heavens. He's nothing like that."

Beneath the lights of the bridge, he had asked her, "You like the Fairchild lady?"

She'd started to ask him how he knew where she worked, then remembered that she was still wearing her badge.

"Her husband paints houses, you know. Used to be wed to the Chamberlain woman."

She hadn't said anything. She'd watched him replace the lid of his pram, testing it firmly to see it was shut. As he shuffled on, having spoken no further, his head had bobbed again through the night.

At lunch, she and Bea carried cafeteria food back along the corridor to the ward. Eleanor only picked at her tray. It reminded her of school lunches in youth: foul-smelling things she'd been forced to consume. Precious they'd considered her there, swapping a tray of kidney pie for an apple.

"What does your husband do, Bea?" she inquired.

The older woman ate soup, cottage cheese. Her appetite was larger than Eleanor's was.

"You mean other than watching TV? Well, he drinks beer. He eats crisps. From time to time he still paints a house." She laughed. "Oh, he's all right. If he made more I mightn't have got into nursing. So at least I can thank him for our being poor."

Months passed. The sea, dark gray through the winter, grew paler blue and was still on its surface. Eleanor's eyes ran with salt mist and pollen; she bought herself short dresses in town.

In time, she stopped regarding the phone. She did not wait with dread for bad news of her mother, or with hope of hearing that she had returned.

One evening, at home, she was smoking the last few crumbs of her grass rolled up in paper when she heard a hollow knock at the door.

"Who is it?" she said, standing at once, waving a hand through the smoke in the air.

"The tooth fairy," came a voice through the door. She heard a body shift in the frame. "It's Deegan. Kirb-acious. Open up, Ellie, would you?"

She did so, relieved to see Deegan Kirby awaiting her with good-natured impatience.

"Paranoia?" he said.

He'd grown a mustache, which suited his face. He was dressed demurely in a T-shirt and short pants, the latter stained with flecks of blue paint.

"I thought you might be Mr. Brevik," she said.

"And you, my dear, have been a little bit naughty." He made a show of sniffing the air. "He wouldn't evict you, but open a window: it positively reeks in the hall."

Beside the table, he picked up what was left of the grass, lit it, and helped himself to a toke.

"Don't worry," he said, catching her face. "I promise, I can get you some more."

Eleanor blushed. "Sit down," she said. "Would you like anything?"

"I wouldn't dream of imposing." He took a seat on the sofa. "Unless you have beer. Or whiskey. Or gin."

"I don't drink, I'm afraid."

He shrugged. "Then I'll have what you're having."

She filled a glass at the tap.

"I'm afraid I haven't got a telly," she said.

"I haven't either. I listen to Ridgewe's."

They talked about his dull work, his love of the stage. He made jokes. Once or twice, she nearly mentioned her mother but dreaded the somber mood that would follow.

Obliquely, he referred to his own past, the distant place he'd grown up. He told about the unending flatiron landscape, the storms that rolled through with violence and speed.

"They were quaint, churchy people. They tried to be kind. They treated me rather like the kid with the clubfoot, or the deaf mute who lived on my road." He laughed.

"I was born here," she said. "But I grew up at school. My parents were almost strangers to me."

He frowned and regarded her flat. "You keep it tidy," he said.

It was the first time she'd had a visitor there. She told him that and then looked away. In the room were a small shelf of books, a cassette deck, her desk, the photograph of her mother. On the wall beside the door to the toilet hung a calendar depicting a horse.

"Do you find yourself lonely?"

She didn't know. "I think perhaps I'm not that kind of person."

He nodded.

"I'm used to being alone."

"So am I."

"I'm sorry about the smell in the hallway."

"Oh, I don't mind. I'm grateful, in fact. We've had such oppressive sobriety here." He took another toke from the grass. "And in any event, Mrs. Ridgewe stinks worse than you ever could. Those horrible fish every morning."

She laughed; she'd begun to feel rather stoned. "Now who's the one being naughty," she said.

SHE PASSED THE old man, on the street or the strand. From a distance, she would recognize him, but he never knew her until they were close. Saturdays, he was in line at the church; the baker offered him stale or burned rolls. Once she saw him trying to fish; twice she saw him eat from a bin. At home, thoughts of him preoccupied her, over dinner or when she was trying to sleep.

She came upon him in front of the bank. People milled about, awaiting tables at Hyde Pantry. She scrawled a note and handed it to him.

I can feed you on Wednesday at Mercy, it said, the day chosen because Beatrice had meetings at noon, and instinctively Eleanor knew Beatrice wouldn't approve.

And so he came to the courtyard where families gathered to visit their sick. She was waiting for him there with a tray. He took it. There was lunch enough only for one, and he did not ask her about that, perhaps having guessed that she was giving him hers. There was ice cream. He ate it and wiped his hands on his trousers, then peeled back the lid on a tin of fruit salad. One of his feet was touching the pram, his toe lifted up and propped on a wheel. In that posture he resembled a father out for an afternoon at the park, his foot there to hold a napping child in place, or to worry it gently if ever it fussed.

"Have you found any treasures lately?" she said.

"Once I found a diamond ring on the strand."

She told how she'd nearly been engaged in the city. He looked up from his tray at her, puzzled.

"Aren't you a Sister?" he said.

She laughed and covered her face with a hand. A heat was rising into her ears, a strange sadness settling into her chest. She knew that she was hurting his feelings, so she gathered herself.

"Have you still got it? The ring, I mean. The one from the strand."

"Turned it in. A person'd hate to lose that." He seemed surprised at the question, surprised she would think he'd done anything else.

"It was good of you."

"I got a reward. Two hundred. I was king for a day."

"Still, it was good."

"Ah, well." His expression was pleased and embarrassed. He said, "The wine merchant, Ault, lets the Gillett boy steal. Did you know that? Wine, whiskey, cigarettes, beer. Hundreds worth he'll have taken by now."

She nodded.

"You don't believe me? He told me. Ault did."

"I do believe you," she said.

"His own son used to bully the Gillett boy. That's back when they were in school. It's the sort of thing that will stay with a person. The Gillett boy had a difficult time."

His tuna sandwich was finished; his apple was chewed to the core.

"Tell me about my mother," she said.

"She's kind. Even though I'm a street person, she is. Mr. Whitaker, she calls me. Never Wen."

"She's left, you know."

"Yes. I miss her," he said.

"How did you meet?"

"She was sometimes unhappy. I'd see her walking in the reeds where I live. People don't often come by that way. Many don't even know it is there. But she did. She would walk there alone. Sometimes I came home and knew she'd been near. She left flowers she'd picked at my door."

"And you talked?"

"Yes. About where she had been. How she'd dreamed of strange creatures, of flying, or music."

Eleanor tried to see them together: fellow travelers of a desolate road, speakers of a dead and beautiful language.

"And do you dream of those things?"

"Yes, of course. Don't you?"

"No. Never. I wish I did."

At the other end of the courtyard, a man in a wheelchair sat in the sun. He shivered a little, delicately, though his dressing gown was thick in the heat. A caretaker sat beside him, reading a book; Eleanor didn't recognize her. Closer to them were a man and a woman: they spoke in whispers; the woman was crying.

He went on. He told about Eleanor's mother dancing ankle-deep in a stream. "Only she could hear the music," he said. "The hem of her dress became heavy with mud."

She wished he'd say more, but his focus meandered; already she felt him drifting away. Soon he turned back to habitual subjects: the spate of weekly reductions at Star, the double feature on for Saturday night.

"I've never been to the pictures myself," he said. "Not for a long time, in any event. Only I like to look at the banners. They're some of them really beautiful things, and some of them very funny as well. Sometimes after a film's run is finished they let me take the banner home in my pram. I'm sure they're as good as the pictures themselves. In many cases I'm certain of that."

AT THE GREENGROCER, they called her Miss Cartwright. She bought food for herself and for her father, knowing he'd otherwise eat TV dinners.

"Good of you, Miss," the greengrocer, Blake, said. "Has there been any word?"

She shook her head.

The fruit buyer was a small, gentle man who spoke little English, being late of Croatia. He showed her how to choose a good melon by pushing against the scar from the vine. Stone fruits he held very close to his face, smiling when she mimicked the act. He said, "Many fruits will soon be in season." Sometimes she saw him at the rear of the market, smoking or chewing at a piece of dry fish. He waved if he saw her, sat up a bit straighter; about him lay empty and broken-down crates, a refuse bin spilling sacks of old food.

"What do you do with turned fruit?" she asked Blake. He was placing her things in a bag.

"Chuck it out if we can't take it home. Or give it away if it isn't too bad."

"Before you chuck it, would you leave it outside? Just on the ground there, next to the bin?"

"I can't be having rodents," he said.

"Only for an hour, I mean. There's someone who'd take it away."

"Wen Whitaker."

"Yes. He eats from the refuse, only it would be nicer for him."

AN INFANT WHO had seemed to be well on the mend took a sudden, sharp turn and died in the ward. A boy. All of it happened so fast; there was not even time to have him moved to the city, where the hospital offered more critical care. When his mother was told, she collapsed to the floor. Eleanor watched her fall in a daze. It seemed the very force of her life had gone out; she might have been a marionette whose strings had of a sudden been cut. She had not been present at the moment of death, and it was that fact she lamented now as she wailed. The father, of weak and youthful appearance, stood aside, struck dumb and fearful as well.

The dead child was mournful and blue. In the last hours it had been too ill to touch.

Only Beatrice remembered herself. She went to the floor beside the broken woman—herself little more than a girl—and touched her without hesitation, gripping her with arthritic hands as firmly as she'd touched the boy in his brief life.

The next morning, Wen Whitaker came.

"I've brought some of my best things to show you."

Eleanor nodded, abstracted and vague. All night she'd lain awake on the floor, Deegan Kirby on the sofa beside her. Sometimes they talked and sometimes he slept. She kept wondering what had been said in the car while that young couple made their way home alone. She'd seen them every day for a week, checked them into the ward, remembered their names, and yet she couldn't begin to imagine. She didn't know them at all.

"I'd fed him," she whispered in the darkness to Deegan. "All last week. With a bottle, I did. More times than his own mother was able."

"I've seen lots of people die," Deegan said.

She was quiet.

"It's strange. They were all of them grown, but they looked exactly the way you've described it. They all looked so dreadfully young."

Now, in the courtyard, Wen Whitaker spoke.

"This is a hairbrush I found near the creek," he said. "The backing is made of a shell. Now what do you suppose it was doing down there?"

"I couldn't say."

"And this is a ribbon I got. There used to be a shop here that sold them," he said.

She felt as if she might weep. It was time she was going back in. She said so, looking down at her watch, and then, without quite knowing why, she began to detail the work she performed, the smallest things: the changing of sheets, the rearrangement of files.

She told about the ache in the arch of her foot, how Beatrice said to be firm with her touch.

"We soothe them," she said, describing the soft, translucent skin, the strained fingers, the way their bodies calmed in her arms.

Wen Whitaker lifted his head. For the first time in their acquaintance, he looked directly into Eleanor's eyes.

"They're born prematurely, you know. They ought still to be in the womb. Beatrice says it's like they're in pain. Every moment they aren't touched, they're in pain."

SUMMER CAME, AND with it a trickle of tourists. Some weekend days she walked by the sea. Children ate candy or swam in the surf. Lovers held hands and made for the shadows, but she did not feel envious of them.

With Deegan she sat, eating mussels in wine.

"I've gotten quite good with the infants," she said. "I'm not frightened to touch them these days."

He nodded but didn't reply. Elsewhere, a clatter when something was dropped. He was drinking his second glass of Chablis. Behind him, the sun had dipped in the sky; the water resembled an orange's peel.

He'd been downcast of late; she didn't know why. Sometimes, as if for no reason at all, a sadness seemed to descend over him. On the bus across town he'd mostly been quiet; through the marina on the way to the restaurant he had frowned at the beaches and parks: mothers photographing their babies, men and women sunning themselves. Her own moods were scarcely strong enough to be felt, a low hum of sorrow, or gladness, or fear.

He covered his face with his hands. At the edges of his nails and the cracks of his cuticles, red and sometimes blue varnish remained.

"Deegan," she said.

He parted his hands.

"Only I wanted to ask: How would it be if I saw your revue?"

He was silent a moment, closing his eyes. For the first time, she wondered how old he might be. Sixty, perhaps. It made her feel sad.

"You don't want to see it," he said.

"Why? I want to know what it's like."

"Trust me. You don't. It's not any good."

"You're only being modest," she said. "I can hear you when you sing in the shower."

He gave a brief, wan smile. "Stop it," he said.

He had a way of leaving her chastened, aware of how little she'd gleaned of his life, of how little effort she'd made.

"Oh, Eleanor. It's a drag show in Croft. Why on earth would you think it was something to see?"

There were not many people left at the tables. She didn't know what to say. A pelican crossed the line of her vision. When she looked back at Deegan he was watching it, too.

"We used to have great shows," he said. "In the city. We used to have such beautiful shows."

IN THE COURTYARD, children were kicking a ball. A man told his wife he'd forgotten her name. Eleanor struck Wen Whitaker's lighter, gold and engraved, then handed it back.

"Tell me more about my mother," she said.

Always she asked this, and always he obliged. She had learned more about her own mother from him than she had in all the years of her childhood.

He was spreading butter and jam onto crackers, eating them in large, single bites.

"She had a wonderful voice. Still does, I imagine. Sometimes she sang while she walked in the reeds. Like a bird, all warbley and fragile," he said.

"Did she tell you she was going to leave?"

"She talked all the time about flying away. We both did. It was something she dreamed of. Great, white, feathered wings, she described."

Eleanor thought of her mother again: the tangles of black hair twisting about her; the way she would sleep for days at a stretch. What world did she dream of? You couldn't imagine. Perhaps one where Eleanor didn't exist.

Later, when Beatrice returned from her meeting, they set about putting fresh sheets onto cots. Methodically, they moved through the room. Beatrice talked of budget concerns.

"Did you know about Ault?" Eleanor said. She hadn't really been thinking about him. It was just something that had come to her mind. "Only I heard something strange about him."

"Yeah?"

"How he lets the Gillett boy steal. Lets him take what he wants from the shop."

Beatrice stopped. "Who told you that?"

At once, Eleanor felt herself blush. She ran a hand over the top of the sheet, tightened a poorly made hospital fold. "Wen Whitaker told me. Just a dull bit of gossip."

"Whitaker told you that?"

"Yes."

"Crazy bugger."

"I haven't met Ault," Eleanor said.

"Ault? No, I mean Whitaker's crazy. That Gillett stole from everybody. But he's dead. He's been dead for ten years. Killed himself with a rope in the closet."

AUTUMN. A CHILL returned to the air. Vendors packed up their goods on the strand. Children were sent, morose, back to school.

No word arrived of Eleanor's mother. Increasingly, thoughts of her were resigned, the past tense used if ever she was mentioned. She had, it seemed, slipped at last from the known world, the force of her drift overcoming its pull, and the greatest sadness in Eleanor's heart was for the peace they would never now make.

In Specialty Care, days remained busy. Beatrice hummed as she moved through the halls. Wednesdays, Wen Whitaker came, his manner increasing in its solicitude. She could see he had run a comb through his hair, that he'd made an effort at cleaning his hands.

One afternoon, he accepted his food but did not right away begin eating. He sat silently, rather, moving his mouth, searching for the form of a word. Did she remember about the babies, he said. What she had explained about them.

She scarcely did. "I'm not sure," she said.

"I wonder is it something I might attempt? Soothing the infants, that is. How you said about soothing the infants with touch."

His hands and his face were trembling, both, with the effort of having said what he had. She regarded the deep lines in his cheeks, the white stubble dotting his jaw and his throat. His eye was clouded just like her father's. In his madness he had danced with her mother.

"The thing is, I've been thinking about it," he said. "Ever since what you told. I think it's a beautiful thing. You said a person might volunteer."

Her first thought was that she would have to convince Bea. He was a kind, gentle man when you knew him.

The next instant, however, reason prevailed, and she saw that of course it couldn't be done. It simply wouldn't do. That was all. His odor was sour and warm. He shifted and shook whenever he moved. If he was seen about Specialty Care, his presence would cause alarm and distress.

"Is it because of the rubbish?" he asked. "I wouldn't pick it up anymore. I wouldn't have any need of the rubbish if only I had a position."

"It isn't the rubbish," she said.

"I'm not a vagrant, if that's what you think."

He spoke now with great agitation, his fingers striking invisible keys.

"Before you decide, let me show you my house. It's good. It has electrical lights."

Slowly, the hope faded out of his voice. He bent over, weeping now into his hands. All these many months they had spoken. *Tell me about my mother*, she'd said. Not once had she asked about his: the touch of her, the way she had been. Never would Eleanor visit

his house near the marsh or see there the items of his meager inher-
itance: a pair of scissors, a spool of white thread, a book in which
his mum had written her name. Blithely, she'd spoken of the pain
of neglect, of being alone, untouched, unbelonging. As if he didn't
already know. As if he weren't sitting right there, within reach.

THEN YEARS PASSED. Eleanor turned thirty-five. Her life
seemed to steady further about her. She took correspondence
courses in nursing, enrolled in the night school, stood for exams;
on the day she received her certification, Beatrice baked her a
chocolate cake. Deegan Kirby stopped by of an evening, albeit
somewhat less frequently now. He was getting older, she saw;
increasingly, he fell asleep on the couch, and she was obliged to
guide him back to his rooms. Mrs. Ridgewe, against all expecta-
tion, met a man and was married, moving to Payne.

Her mother was spotted in Wexford, then Brill, heading north
in each instance, hitching a ride. Her long, black hair had begun
to turn white, chopped roughly short as if with a saw, but her
eyes—pale and haunted—had matched the reports.

"Let her go, button. It's for the best," Eleanor's father said. The
sound of his voice was vague, otherworldly, like filaments in a
spent, shaken bulb. "Let her be. She wasn't ever happy in Glass."

And so she carries on in the ward. Restraint and a pleasant,
underwhelming contentment prevail, still, in the affairs of her life.
It is something she has come to accept. Beatrice talks of retirement
often, and the thought of staying on isn't daunting to Eleanor. She
is roiled only on those afternoons when, watching Wen Whitaker
eat, an old longing rises up in her breast.

He never speaks anymore beyond his vague thanks, never moves that she might sit beside him. She knows it isn't pride that prevents him. It isn't anger or passive rebuke. It is shame, only simple, unalloyed shame. Not there when begging from a rabbi or nun—charity being part of their creed—it comes nonetheless in the courtyard of Mercy: the humiliation of asking for food where he wasn't deemed fit to comfort an infant. When he looked up, having taken her for a Sister, there would have been the first pang of it then.

He finishes, wiping his hands on his trousers, and Eleanor turns away from the window. Returning to the floor of the ward, she lifts a child into her arms. It squirms a moment, but she is firm in her embrace. Beatrice is standing there also: unspeaking, they commence with their work, humming tunelessly, deep in their throats, the vibrations being therapeutic as well. It isn't true what her father said, that her mother wasn't ever happy in Glass. Surely she was as she danced through a stream, the hem of her dress growing heavy with mud, or as she collected fresh flowers to lay at the doorstep of a secret companion. She wishes now she had asked Wen, *Did you love her?* but feels also that she already knows. That language of strange dreams and found treasure: what is that but a language of love? And what was it, for that matter, when he brought her a hairbrush, when he showed it to her, strands of black hair (or has she only imagined it?) trailing delicately from its bristles?

The realm of human love is as large as an ocean, she thinks, and she is somebody tracing the shore.

At the Circus

✕ ✕ ✕

In the restaurant, people were eating alone. At small tables next to the windows they were. Tony watched them, the steam that rose from their mugs, and wondered how it would be to grow up, to eat in a restaurant whenever you liked. He felt he would do it every day. This one was called Big Buddy Boy Brown. In the car park, when first they'd arrived, he had managed to read the words on the sign. Mr. Avery said it was grand. He liked the mural of a dog wearing trousers, the chairs around the tables that swiveled in place. They were painted bright red and shiny, the chairs. The tables were made to resemble real wood.

"Drink a bit more of your milk, Tony, will you?"

Mr. Avery handed the carton to him.

You ordered your breakfast from a man at a counter, and then it was given to you on a tray. His breakfast was intended for children. He had chosen it on Mr. Avery's suggestion. "When I was your age, I ate the Buddy Boy Biscuit," he'd said, and Tony hadn't objected. When he was older, he would eat a more mature sort of breakfast, and he would order a soft drink as well.

"You need the energy," said Mr. Avery now.

Tony didn't really want the milk, but he drank it. In truth, he did not like his food very much. The biscuit was really rather more like a scone; it was cold in the center, and so was the egg. Still, it was special to be in a restaurant. Aunt Beryl didn't care for going out much herself.

"If you don't want the rest of your breakfast, that's all right. Only have the milk, Tony. That's a good boy."

Mr. Avery's own breakfast hadn't been finished. On the orange tray there were scraps cast aside.

Next to the window a fat man was eating. He had an enormous pile of hot cakes.

"The circus will be grand," Mr. Avery said. "It's a long time since I saw one myself."

Tony nodded, wiping milk from his lips. Mr. Avery's hair had grown over his ears; his clothes were tatty at the collars and cuffs.

"Are the clowns very funny?"

"Marvelous. Yes."

Mr. Avery liked taking Tony to things. As a boy, he had been keen on the circus. He'd told all about the acrobats and the lions.

"When I went I had never seen something so good."

Outside, Tony felt a lifting of spirits.

"That was a very good breakfast," he said, thinking of the brown dog wearing trousers and of swiveling back and forth in the chair. At school he would tell Joey Makepeace about it. He would tell Harriet Aldridge as well. "This is a great restaurant, I'd say."

"It was always a favorite of mine."

He looked up at Mr. Avery, the smile on his face, his head tilted up toward the sun. He had known this older man all of his life, though if asked, he could not have said how. When you didn't have a mother or father, people took an interest in you. It was a kindness, one you mustn't turn back.

"Gosh, your mother was an angel," Mr. Avery said, as he had done also on other occasions, always when Aunt Beryl wasn't around. She never talked about Tony's mother and would not have liked Mr. Avery to. "The loveliest woman I've met in my life." His face became somber as always it did, and he turned it away from the sky. "Don't ever listen if someone contradicts that, Tony. It's a lie if somebody does."

BERYL BIDEFORD HUNG the wash on the line. A low sun fell in weak, canted shafts upon the bare skin of her arms and throat. The garden—unkempt and left to grow wild—was just beginning to turn with the year; she moved through it with neither languor nor haste, pleased with its savage, riotous look. Clothing and linens she pinned at one end, underthings where they were hidden from view. In earlier years she would not have bothered concealing her knickers, might even have enjoyed the idea that a neighbor boy or a frustrated husband would see them and later have a wank in her honor, but now, at fifty, she'd have found it unseemly. Time changed you in that way, and others.

Autumn sea air swept up and over the hills, cooling the damp, heavy fabric she hung. After this, there was the kitchen to sweep, a sweater button to mend for the boy. Nothing else, though: she'd otherwise be at leisure. No supper to cook, no piss on the bog seat; a mercy, his being out for the day. For a meal she would eat whatever was on hand: sardines, or something else tinned. She would drink tea and sherry with her feet on the sofa, not obliged for once to set an example.

Beneath her, where the hill fell away, beyond the roofs of neighboring homes, a skiff turned around in the harbor. She watched it, thinking of sailors and gin.

The fact was, she felt herself too old for parenthood, and ill-suited besides. You'd be hard-hearted not to care for the boy, but that didn't mean the domestic life suited. She'd been glad to have Avery take him, despite her ample misgivings. No sense in denial: the man was a drunk. But you needed a day here and there to yourself, and you couldn't refuse the child a friend. Least of all one whose intentions were good. She had known Joe Avery a great many years, long before he fell into ruin.

The kitchen smelled of a ginger detergent, the space lighted even in its westerly aspect. Beyond it, the living room lay in darkness, the curtains pulled-to against the brightening day. She put the kettle on and, while it boiled, went through to set a log in the grate. A lamp beside the sofa gave a fragile, warm light, enough to illuminate the page of a book.

On the mantel, reflecting the first licks of flame, were two obelisks carved of black stone. They had been a gift from Mr. Rutherford Townes, a contractor with the Raleigh concern. Years ago, he had put forth a bid for repaving the Payne Road, and she had seen that the council accepted. Indispensable Beryl had been considered at work. That word had often been used. Other things in the house had been similarly gifted: a necklace, an ashtray, a pair of glass bookends.

Her tea cooled. The fire grew and took hold. It was pleasant, giddy, having the run of the house. The kitchen floor could wait until evening. It could even be put off for a day.

Reclining luxuriously, she remembered the Champagne that evening with Townes. His large hands, his laugh when they toasted themselves. She remembered the power she'd held over him—in her offices and at the Cavalry later; in each instance she had granted his wish only because it had been her wish as well.

A bus ticket marked the page in her book, the latest romance in a series she liked. Vi at the library kept them on order. "Another steamy one, dear," she would say. "You'll need a smoke after this one. Don't burn the sheets." The books were all that remained of Beryl's old life, chapters stolen while the boy was at school or in the night if he slept long enough to allow it. In the past the term *old maid* had amused her, as pity had when offered to her. She had laughed at what people were ignorant of. It was the same pleasure she took when men would enter her office, condescending because of her title. *Secretary*, it had said on her desk, even though it was she who'd held the key to the city.

The logs shifted and she rose to adjust them. All that had ended with the advent of the boy, when she'd had to leave work with a derisory pension. Still, she was careful never to blame him; he'd be the last one she held to account. Blame fell, if anywhere, with her sister. With Pearl, who had left him alone in the world.

In the novel a farmer tore a fruit in his hands. The heroine bit the flesh from the stone. Townes had been somewhat unlike the others, because even months after the Payne Road was finished he had called her on the telephone, evenings, had asked to see her at the Cavalry Inn. Others had professed to be injured or shocked when they learned she had no interest in marriage, but Townes had said only, "Then I'll take what's on offer."

The girl in the book would fall in love with the farmer, a foolishness Beryl lightheartedly scorned. "A roll and a stroll" her own motto had been. Perhaps nature, she thought, had divided things such that Pearl entertained love enough for them both. Certainly that would seem to have been so. Heaven knew the poor dear had never been above folly.

THE CIRCUS WAS held beneath a great tent. A big top, Mr. Avery called it. It had white and red stripes up its length. From the field where they parked, some distance away, it resembled a giant peppermint sweet; Mr. Avery said so and Tony agreed.

"Perhaps you'll have a peppermint candy of your own. They have large sticks that will last the whole day. Would you like that, Tony? A peppermint sweet?"

Tony shrugged and pressed an ear to his shoulder, a habit because the wool of his sweater was soft.

"Or is it another you're thinking about? You can have whatever you like. It's not every day you go to the circus."

"And I ate a good breakfast."

"Aye. That you did. So which is it? Which treat did you fancy?"

They crossed a bridge over the roadway they'd traveled and another empty lot at the edge of the fairground. Other children walked with their parents, holding hands or sometimes running ahead.

"I was thinking of candy floss, really."

He'd been told about the pink and pillowy sweet, how it vanished as soon as it went in your mouth.

"You'll like that," Mr. Avery said. "It's another favorite of mine."

There were booths set up around the edge of the tent. Clowns were making shapes from balloons. Music played; you couldn't tell where it came from. The same sort you'd hear at the boardwalk in Glass. The clowns wore colorful trousers and shirts, with bright hair beneath their hats and paint on their faces.

"Let's find our seats first," Mr. Avery said. "When we've found them, I can go for the sweets."

"All right."

"Or did you want a balloon? The clowns can make marvelous shapes with balloons."

Tony regarded one of the clowns. He wore ragged clothing and gloves on his hands; beside him, propped against the side of a stall, was a handkerchief on the end of a stick.

He shook his head and they made for the entrance, where ushers in fancy dress stood by the turnstiles.

"Hold on to your ticket," Mr. Avery said, handing Tony a piece of blue paper.

People began pushing as they drew near the entrance. Tony stood at Mr. Avery's side. The clown with the kerchief on the end of a stick had forgotten to paint a bit of his throat. The bare skin had shown, sunburned and stubbled; thinking about it made Tony afraid.

"Step right up," said a man in a hat. He was nearly as big as the one from that morning, by the window eating hot cakes for breakfast.

"You'll hand him the ticket," Mr. Avery said.

Tony nodded. The man tore his ticket in half.

In the big top there was a great deal of noise. Children sat or stood on their seats, shouting and pointing at the still-empty stage. The air was heavy and smelled of wet paper. Tony felt too hot in his sweater. In school it was like this: noisy and savage. At lunchtime, or in the assembly hall. He ate his lunch with Joey Makepeace at the edge of the yard, many days not saying a thing. Joey never asked about Tony's mother, as sometimes other boys rudely did. If Joey talked, it was about a picture he'd seen or about freight lorries, which interested him. He wore eyeglasses and had the large teeth of a rabbit.

Their seats were near the edge of the tent, raised from the ground like gymnasium stands. Beside them were a boy and a girl.

"Wait here," Mr. Avery said. "I'll get our treats and be back in a flash. There's a good ten minutes before it begins."

Tony watched Mr. Avery go. From his seat, the stage appeared distant and small.

A freight lorry might weigh forty tons, Joey said, which was nearly as much as a whale. A hush descended over the tent. Music started playing from speakers, loud drumming, a voice that said, "Ladies and gentlemen." Even the unruly children were still.

From the rafters on either side of the stage, two men began falling, suspended from ropes. Arms spread, as if in flight, they held on with their feet. Acrobats: Tony knew it at once. They swung down in shocking, dangerous arcs. People gasped; a number of children jumped up. Where the acrobats met, they each leaped through the air, catching hold of the other man's rope and swinging to the opposite side of the stage.

Tony had never seen anything like it. He couldn't imagine being so brave. Even from a distance you couldn't believe it. They resembled a kite he'd once seen a man fly: triangular, carving sharp lines in the air.

He had been with Mr. Avery on that day as well, and Aunt Beryl. He had been given a kite of his own, and Aunt Beryl had allowed him to keep it. Sometimes she said he could not accept gifts, but when Mr. Avery gave him the kite she said yes. It was orange and blue, in the shape of a dragon. Aunt Beryl had stood beside Mr. Avery, not speaking much but companionable. Mr. Avery had shown him how you'd wait for a gust, then run with the string taut behind you.

"First time out?" the man with the other kite had asked Tony. When the green triangle turned in the sky it sounded like a piece of cloth being torn.

"A birthday present," Aunt Beryl replied. "From his friend, Mr. Avery here."

After that it had mostly been spoiled. After she had said *friend* to the man. It would not have been so bad to be taken for Mr. Avery's son. Tony wouldn't have minded at all. It would have been all right to be mistaken for a family.

Quickly, he scanned the crowd and the aisles. Mr. Avery couldn't be seen.

Now there were four men swinging from ropes. Each of them tumbled and turned. The music grew louder and faster in pace, and with it the speed of the jumping increased. Everyone cheered as the men flipped about. In the end, they all let go of their ropes and landed with their hands on their hips. The audience carried on with applause.

Another man came onto the stage. He was dressed like the one who had taken the tickets. He began shouting into a speaker. Tony covered his ears. He looked again for Mr. Avery but still didn't see him. He had said he wouldn't miss the start of the show. A clown came out and stood behind the man in the hat, mocking him, aping his movements. When the man turned around, the clown would be still. Everybody in the whole big top laughed.

Tony felt a tap on his shoulder.

"Where's your dad gone?"

It was the girl who was sitting beside him. She wore a blue dress and had brown hair in braids.

In school, Harriet Aldridge was kind. Joey Makepeace said he found her very pretty, but Tony thought he was only saying so. This one was a little bit older. Eight, perhaps even nine.

"He's only gone to buy a candy," he said.

"What kind?"

"Candy floss. I've never had it before."

The girl turned her attention back to the stage, laughing at something the clown had just done. Her brother leaned across their mother's lap. "Eugenia's talking to a stranger," he said.

"He's only a little boy," the girl said. "His father left to buy a treat and he hasn't come back."

"He will come back," Tony said, though his heart was beginning to thump. The heat and the laughter were making it worse.

Eugenia's mother was looking at him. She had stopped paying any attention to the circus.

"All right?" she said, in a delicate voice, and then repeated, louder, because of the noise.

Tony nodded and pretended to look at the stage.

"Your dad's been gone since the start of the show?"

The mother had pale, pudgy skin on her face. It looked like the biscuit he'd eaten for breakfast.

"He only went for a sweet," Tony said.

"Twenty-five minutes it's been."

Aunt Beryl sometimes said you couldn't count on Mr. Avery. He was the kind of man who blew with the wind. "More, even, than most," is what she had said. But still he wouldn't miss the whole show. All morning he had been on about things: The jugglers and clowns. The bear who could dance. The man who put himself in a box. It was only that people were crowding around. That was what was troubling Tony. They were wondering where his father had gone. He was tired of people wondering that, and he was tired of them wondering about his mother as well.

"He's maybe having a cigarette," Eugenia said. "It might be he doesn't like to smoke around kids."

Tears were coming into his eyes. If a fuss was made, things would be spoiled again. Aunt Beryl would see that something was wrong and would say again how you couldn't count on a man. She wouldn't invite him to stay and have tea; she wouldn't be companionable.

"It doesn't matter," Tony said.

He made his hands into fists and pressed them under his eyes, the way Joey Makepeace had said you could do. You put your fists on the tops of your cheeks and pressed there. It was a way to be brave.

"It doesn't matter at all," he repeated. Again, he scanned the crowd for Mr. Avery's face.

WHEN BERYL WOKE, having dozed, she took a moment to gather herself. The light from the lamp beside the sofa was faint; the embers had begun to die down in the grate. She did not know how long she had been sleeping, only that she'd dreamed of rollicking things.

She rose and spent a moment stoking the fire. It leaped to, bringing a flush to her cheeks. In the kitchen, she opened a tin of sardines. The sun, through the windows, had peaked. The wash fluttered lightly where it hung on the line.

In her book, the farmer had proved to be good, but the heroine's father didn't approve. He wanted her to marry a county solicitor, but the girl's youthful passion would not be denied. The farmer knew about the body in a primitive way, in touch as he was with the heavens and earth. It was a ridiculous, sentimental idea, but Beryl indulged it nevertheless. The novel was called *He Worked the Land*. On the cover, a man was holding a peach.

It had crossed her mind to give Townes a ring, to call him up, just out of the blue. That would come as a shock, and he'd say so: "Now this is a pleasant surprise."

She had been the one to break off their relations, seeing the clear direction of things. All the love had gone out of his marriage; increasingly, he talked about that. It might have been a lie, or it might have been true, but in either case she shrunk from what it portended.

If she'd called him today, he'd have come to the house, able to only because he'd been summoned. Of all the afternoons and evenings they'd shared, none had ever been spent at her place. He'd have looked around, sizing it up. The obelisks would have been on the mantel.

"Been thinking about me?" he would have said, lifting his eyebrows with playful suggestion.

How they'd laughed in later days at that odd, phallic gift! "I had designs on you; that I confess," he had said. "But I didn't mean anything by it." They had been side by side on the starched hotel bedding; it was after the first time. In the heat, she looked over his body and, gently taking him up in her hand, said, "I had a scare when I opened the box, what with there being the two of them there. I didn't know what you were on to!"

If he'd come today, she might have repeated that joke. Ribaldry was something each of them liked.

In the end, of course, she hadn't called because of the boy. With Joe, things were bound to go wrong at the circus: his car might break down; he might lose the tickets; he might make the boy sick by feeding him sweets. She laughed as she pictured the scene there'd have been then: Townes in the bedroom when they returned, his white rump exposed as he turned to the wall. A part of her would enjoy such a thing.

When she said it was over, he'd looked at the ground. He'd taken his woolen hat in his hands. She knew he was only pretending to suffer, or was anyway exaggerating his pain. His large head fell from heavy, stooped shoulders. It was a kindness, or he meant it as one.

"From the first day, you were something different," he'd said. "'A force to be reckoned with,' I said to myself."

She smashed the sardines onto pieces of toast, picking away the pebbly bones. They might equally have gone to the Cavalry Inn. That would have been one for old times. She'd have ordered a sherry and a whiskey for him, remembering the type he preferred.

"Still queen of the parish offices, then?" he'd have asked, hanging his hat on the rack. He'd have taken her coat and hung that as well. Then she'd have had to tell him the truth.

EVERYBODY WAS STANDING around. They were watching Tony as he talked to the man.

"Well it's not even been the whole of an hour. Could be he can't remember your seat. Could be he dropped his ticket someplace."

It was the man who had torn the ticket outside. The top of his head was shiny and damp; wispy gray hairs clung to his scalp.

"All the same," said Eugenia's mother, "you could page him."

Tony was aware of people closing around him. The trick where you held your fists to your cheeks had stopped working after a while, and he felt the tears where they'd run on his face. It was all spoiled: people would pity him now.

"Oh, we'll do that. Just before the start of the next act. Let's give him a few minutes more."

Eugenia came and stood next to Tony. "You mustn't be worried," she said.

"I don't like people looking at me."

"Oh," she said, "I know what you mean. My mother is always making a show."

Her brother came and stood next to them, too.

"We could go looking, Ma," the boy said, but just then Tony saw Mr. Avery.

He was making his way through the crowd, just a head bobbing up between others at first. He moved quickly, perhaps sensing he'd been a long time; he bumped into people, excusing himself. Tony jumped up and down when he saw him. He was holding a pink cloud of candy aloft.

"That's him," Tony shouted. "I said he would come."

"All's well that ends well," the ticket man said.

Mr. Avery smiled as he approached, a sheepish grin, too big for his face. His eyes scanned the seats where people had gathered, flitting from Tony to Eugenia's mother.

"Ah, I've made it. Gosh, what a crowd." He put an arm around Tony's shoulders and squeezed.

The space around them remained very close.

"What's this?" Mr. Avery said. "Tears? Were you very upset? Only it took a longer time than I thought."

He offered the candy and Tony accepted. When you held it, it weighed almost nothing at all.

"Come on, then. What did I miss?"

With his free hand, Tony wiped the tears from his face. "The acrobats. And a bit with the clowns."

People were still looking at them.

"Was it very good?" Mr. Avery said. "Acrobats are amazing, I think."

Eugenia's mother was shaking her head.

"They swung on ropes," Tony replied.

"Ah, that would be the trapeze. I must say I'm sorry to have missed the trapeze."

They sat down. On the stage, the lights had grown dim. Tony turned the candy floss in his hand. It was pink. He hadn't thought he wanted a sweet, but now he took as large a bite as he could. It was sticky, and it vanished on the end of his tongue exactly as he had been told it would do.

"Is it good, Tony?"

He said that it was.

On Mr. Avery's neck drops of sweat could be seen. His hair was matted as the ticket man's had been. He ran a finger along the inside of his collar.

When the music began for the high-wire act, Mr. Avery turned and smiled again. He patted Tony twice on the knee.

Beside him, Eugenia's mother was frowning. In his mind he said a curse about her. She hadn't been as kind as Eugenia had; it had been she who'd started the fuss. It was because of that that he forgave Mr. Avery, to show that everything was all right. Without speaking, he handed some candy to Eugenia, who took it and put it into her mouth. Her brother reached a hand over her lap, and Tony gave him a little bit, too. They were at the circus with only that woman. Nobody asked whether she was their mother. Nobody asked where their father had gone.

AROUND SEVEN, BERYL poured a small glass of sherry. At the table she ran a hand through her hair. For a man, there was Joe Avery, of course. She thought about that with mild distaste. He would not have the strength of Rutherford Townes, or the bawdy, lighthearted way with her after, but she knew that if she resigned herself to him, he'd resign himself in a similar way. This evening he might, or any time in the future. She had only to make up her mind. Such a thing wouldn't offer either one of them joy, but the knowledge of its being to hand was a comfort: it made it so that solitude was something you chose.

One afternoon, some eight or ten years ago, she had run into her sister in Glass. She'd stopped in for coffee and a bite after work and saw Pearl seated in a booth by the window, laughing with another one of her men. Her youth was like a fine silk or fur she might wear without any notion of what it had cost. For some moments, at first, she didn't see Beryl; she was perfectly unaffected and calm. And for those moments Beryl loved her sister, more than ever before or after. She didn't begrudge Pearl the fun she was having: being taken out, called late at night on the phone. Joe Avery was hopeless for Pearl in those days, buying flowers, stopping for tea unannounced—an old-fashioned courtship to which Pearl condescended—but just then any hopes of his seemed absurd.

When she looked up and saw Beryl, Pearl said, "You must join us."

The young man she sat with was shiftless and thin. He turned an unlit cigarette in his fingers; from time to time he glanced at the window. Pearl said his name was Hubert, giving it a French pronunciation: *Ooh-bear.*

"I really can't stay very long," Beryl said.

"Rushing off, are you? A date, is it, Beryl?"

Pearl laughed, and Beryl only smiled a bit, because in fact she was going to the Cavalry Inn. Such a strange child, Pearl—unimaginable—to be at once so naive and so tarty.

"We're half sisters," she explained to Hubert.

Later, Beryl had thought of that day—the man's disinterested, indolent manner; the slant of his forehead; the flick of his eyes. She had looked for those things in the face of the boy but never found them; it might have been anyone else.

When she was leaving, having had her coffee and food, Beryl heard Pearl say, "Poor old Sissy," and laugh.

The superiority, the pity one feels toward the dying: in her extreme youth, Pearl had felt these toward the world. You couldn't be angry. Not really. Not, at least, so long as you had your own life. The trouble was how, in death, Pearl had made of Beryl precisely what she'd assumed her to be.

The floor, unswept, was mockingly there. The high spirits of the morning had sunk. She poured herself another small glass of the wine.

Pride, too, made a strike against Avery: she didn't want any more of Pearl's leavings. You made your own way, as best as you could, hoarding memories like lost teeth or old gowns, a space saved inside for the person you'd been: unafraid, unrepentant in a bed by the sea, the body ecstatic, celebrating itself.

IN THE CAR on the way home from the circus, Mr. Avery talked about what they had seen.

"How do you think the man fit in that box?" he said. "Could you credit that, Tony?"

Outside the window the sky had grown dark. Tony was feeling sick from his sweets and from the sausage roll he'd eaten after the circus. They didn't speak about the fact that he'd cried, both feeling embarrassed about it.

Along the side of the road there were lights in the distance: villages, maybe, or the edge of the sea. In the mirror you could tell where the big top had been, a glowing bit of sky surrounded by blackness. For a while Tony stopped paying attention, simply letting the texture of the night hurry past, the air from the window, the hum of the road. In his ears, the carnival music played on. The long day presented itself, and he watched it unfold as if from afar. He was thinking of the clown with a handkerchief and a stick when he heard what Mr. Avery said: "If I could go back and be a child, I would. In a second. No question about it. I would."

The older man gripped the wheel and stared intently ahead, making small corrections when he drifted or turned.

"Your mother was a lovely woman, you know. A girl, really. Hardly more than a girl. Have you ever wondered what she was like?"

Tony's heart began to feel low. Sometimes, without any warning at all, the image of her would appear in his dreams. He had never been told how it was that she'd died, but in his vision she was drowned in the sea. He knew from pictures that she had fair hair and eyes, and it was that hair, suspended like gauze in the water, that always woke him with a shuddering start.

"She had a sweet nature. Wonderfully so. Even though she didn't want me to court her, she let me come and have a chat now and then. It never changed things, the troubles she had. I was never any different with her. Only think if she could look at us now. Only think. She might even be pleased."

Tony closed his eyes and pretended to sleep, his head near to Mr. Avery's arm.

By the time they reached home there was a chill in the air. Aunt Beryl had left the porch light on. She met them in the front room when they entered, the door not having been locked.

"Did you boys have fun at the circus?"

You could see at once that she was feeling suspicious. She examined Mr. Avery's face.

"We saw the trapeze and a man in a box," Tony said, rushing into the house. "And I made friends with a boy and a girl, and I ate sweets and sausage and a Buddy Boy Biscuit."

He shouted when he told Aunt Beryl those things, wanting her to feel he had liked them.

"And come home with vim and vigor to spare," she said. "Not planning on sleeping, I guess?"

Mr. Avery still hadn't said anything. He stood in the doorway, regarding his feet. At length, he said, "He's a very good boy."

Tony paused by the door to the kitchen. The room smelled of ginger and woodsmoke and ash.

"I will go to sleep, Auntie Beryl," he said. "I'm tired as a matter of fact."

He brushed his teeth and put on his pajamas himself. If he was good, she might let Mr. Avery stay. It might help his spirits to stay for a while.

He could hear them in the living room while he dressed, talking, perhaps companionably. He heard the kettle go on, and that made him happy; he smiled as he climbed into bed. Again the men swung down on their ropes; again Eugenia's voice said *your dad*. Hidden in his closet, in a small paper sack, were the last few sticky pieces of candy. Mr. Avery had found the sack in his car so that Tony could save a little to share. He would bring it to school Monday morning. Everyone would be jealous of him.

As sleep overtook him, he heard a voice, faintly. "Goodnight, boyo," it said. "That was grand."

BERYL STOOD ON one side of the threshold; Joe Avery stood on the other. The glare from the porch light was harsh on his features, shadowed when moths flitted over the bulb.

"It's good of you, Joe," she said. "Despite everything."

"Do you think he had a good time?"

On the sofa, while he finished his tea, she had watched him, the teacup small in his hands. He was shaven and washed and not terribly drunk: he'd made that effort today. She was grateful for it, admiring even, but still she didn't want him to stay.

"Maybe you can fix yourself up," she said now. "This dirt on your collar, these stains. Bring your wash over. I've got a machine."

Slowly, he made his way to the car, his bent and ponderous figure. At the driver's side door, he paused to light a cigarette, exhaling the smoke in the air. It had been he who'd found Pearl's body that day, draped loosely, at an angle, over the bedspread. At first he had thought it was only a dress, a mere twist of fabric, carelessly thrown.

His headlights cast a pale glow on the drive; his tires noisily crunched over gravel. Loving the mother, he loved the son, too. It was natural to him that he should. A painful thing, calling him back to the past, but there was the restoration of something as well.

In the house, Beryl stirred up the last of the embers. Her book had been locked away in a drawer.

They were all three of them orphans. That thought occurred now, as it hadn't before. Each one bereft of a different love in one common stroke of youthful caprice. Sharing that was something for her. It was something for Joe Avery, too. In their lives they had that much, at least. Later, for the boy, there would be other things, but for now you knew enough to take what there was.

Virginia's Birthday

)X)X)X

Sunday nights along the boardwalk are slow: locals retired, weekenders gone. By midnight, the Blue Parrot has emptied. Tables lie unoccupied in front of the stage upon which May Valentine sings with the band. Where guests dined, candles flicker and die, a highball has here or there been abandoned. Above the piano, catching the light, turns the pale, bluish smoke from Ham's cigarette. A number ends, "The Nearness of You," and from his place, sitting at the rear of the club, Walter Chapman applauds, alone in the shadows.

It is a painful evening for Walter. Every week Sunday evening is painful. The club is not open on Monday or Tuesday, and the knowledge that he will not see May in that time makes it so. He watches her now, draped in a shimmering fabric like water: here pooling, here running over hipbone or breast. Her skin is deep brown, pearls iridescent beside it. He has loved her since the day in 1954 when she answered his first-ever call for auditions. "Stardust." Another Hoagy Carmichael tune. Not thirty, already she sang with a wisdom; her references told of an itinerant past (London, Amsterdam, Montreal). Mr. Chapman is what she called him that day, and has continued to call him the better part of two decades since.

The band starts again, "You Go to My Head." The arrangement, like all their arrangements, is sparse. Once soft-textured and warm, May's voice has begun to grow brittle of late. Sometimes, summoned for a bend or a pickup, it strains and then cracks like a bird's hollow bone. Walter doesn't mind. The fragility suits her. She always had a gift for turning a phrase as if it took all the strength in her body to do it. The suggestion was of privacy, solitude; you couldn't help but fall in love when you heard it, and now, even knowing she does not love him back, it is a comfort and consolation to him. The band plays, Walter has caught himself thinking, with the frail, haunted beauty of a burned-out home: the rhythm section—discordant and lurching—like high ruined rafters and walls, through the cracks in which Posey's trumpet emerges, a shaft of light, the mere suggestion of a note in his breath, and around which May's voice has twisted itself, like the bright, tattered silk of a scarf—not undamaged but somehow, miraculously, spared—lifted on an updraft of fiery air.

After the set, he finds her alone in her dressing room. He knocks, though he knows she will not be indecent. She never changes her clothes in the club.

She regards herself in the mirror, not appraisingly but with resignation, with boredom. The pins have already been removed from her hair.

"It was a good show. You sounded good, May."

"If only someone had been there to see it." She pours a drink: gin, kept among her perfumes.

"Sunday night," Walter says. He watches her swallow. Her lips leave another red stain on the glass.

"I'm glad you liked the show, Mr. Chapman."

She does not invite him to sit, does not offer to pour him a drink. When she speaks, she addresses his reflection in the mirror. She closes her eyes and with the pads of her fingers massages the skin about her temples and jaw.

"Birthday's coming up," he says. "She excited?"

"Virginia? I imagine she is."

Each year at the club there is a small celebration: gifts and a cake. The band plays something special.

"Sweet sixteen."

"That's right." She plucks a stray hair from her brow. "Thursday. And every bit of it, too. Just last week she failed an exam. Algebra. Chemistry, maybe. It used to be she was top of the class."

"She's a good girl," he says. "She'll do well on the next one. Seems no time ago she would come round the club."

May used to be apologetic about it, but he never minded the girl. He enjoyed bringing her soft drinks and pretzels, playing jacks or pinochle while her mother performed. He gave her crayons and pens to draw pictures with, stamps that she pasted into a book.

"Doesn't it?" May says now, abstracted. "I rather think it does seem a long time. Some days it feels like a million years."

MAY ARRIVES HOME after two in the morning, having stayed for a drink with Al at the bar and then hitched a ride with him back to the city. Virginia is asleep on the sofa, the TV left on with the test pattern showing. She does not stir when the screen is shut off, as she didn't either when May had to fuss with the door. May knows that Virginia takes drugs. The kids at school must have gotten her on to them. Pills, maybe: she hasn't smelled drink or reefer. It worries her to think about that, and because it does she brings over a blanket. It is spring, but the nights are still cold, and the window in the bathroom doesn't properly close. In the darkness, Virginia looks peaceful. May would like to sit for a while—a girl needs her mother, she knows—but it is so late, and she makes her way instead to the bedroom, from beneath the door of which there comes no trace of light.

She undresses and slides herself under the covers. "Move over, old lady," she almost says in a whisper, as if she'd forgotten that Agnes is gone.

She runs a hand along the sheet where once a warm body slept. Agnes always took more than her share of the bed, but May never minded that very much. If she were here now, Agnes might reach out to touch her, she might pull her into a folded embrace.

"Did you sing nice tonight?" May hears her say. Agnes used to ask her that every night.

"Yes. We did 'The Nearness of You.'"

Sometimes she still finds traces of Agnes: small hairs in a comb, her scent in a scarf. After three months that is all that remains. Soon, she thinks, there will be nothing at all.

"Of course, there was hardly a soul in the place."

They met in a tea shop. Outside was a hailstorm; Agnes had come seeking shelter. She was dressed far too lightly for winter, a trench coat over a thin cotton dress. The first woman May had seen with natural hair. It was cropped short. Her face was angular, stern, a strength in it that was somehow recalled in the extreme narrowness of her wrists and her hands. Later, May would wonder at that, the power contained in that willowy frame. When Agnes reached for her in the night, her grip was sometimes overwhelmingly strong.

"I'm a singer," May said, when they spoke in the shop. "A jazz singer as a matter of fact."

Agnes said, "I'm keen on church music, myself."

The hail abated and gave way to hard rain, which ran down the windows behind them in sheets. Headlamps from cars could be seen from the street, washed out, indistinct, like jewels glimpsed in water.

"Do you believe in God?" Agnes said, and May admitted she didn't. "That's all right. Sometimes love can take time."

They lived together eight years.

In the darkness, May says, "He's sure to go under. I don't know how he's managed this long."

There is comfort in speaking aloud.

"Did Virginia finish her homework tonight? Agnes, do you think she takes drugs?"

In the living room, Virginia lifts her head from the pillow. Like a strange, ghostly detail from a dream, she recalls her mother having been in the room. The keys in the lock, the television switched off: these sounds register after the fact. The pills she took are stronger than the previous ones. Jeanene has warned her of that. She doesn't know what is in them; Jeanene doesn't either. They make you feel like you are taking a bath. Whatever the color, that's the name of the pill: red, blue, yellow, or pink.

Another sound emerges, more immediate now. It is her mother's voice, a murmur from under the door. She is talking to Agnes again; knowing that, Virginia feels sorry for her. These months they have suffered apart, not able in their grief to comfort each other. Fly-by-night is what May called the man Agnes left with. Virginia could not recall having seen him. There had been people who came and went through the years, new congregants and preachers who guided her spirit. She was the sort of person always searching for something; a holy fool, May sometimes said. But nights, when they were alone, she would tenderly braid Virginia's hair. They would laugh at stories of childhood mischief, old jobs from which Agnes had got herself sacked. When first she'd come to live in their flat May had called her Virginia's aunt. But Agnes never made any mention of that. Standing over steaming pots in the kitchen, she explained the proper way to make curry, or soup, having been taught in just the same way as a girl.

It would not have changed anything, the truth being spoken. Things would have been better, in fact. She does not mind that her mother is that way. It doesn't matter at all. She only wishes there had been no pretense, that she might have loved Agnes unfettered by lies. Sometimes Fergie Davidson says things about it, and about Mr. Chapman as well. At school, people say Fergie fancies Virginia. That's why he hurts her feelings so much. Four Eyes he used to call her. Lemonade because her complexion was pale. Lately he has begun to say other things, things that make her scalp itch with discomfort: "What's two and six buy me? Three? Have a heart. I'll starve. You drive a hard bargain, Missy."

"There was wickedness here," Agnes said when she left, and Virginia knows that was painful for May. She wouldn't have been in her right mind to say that. It would have been a madness, speaking that way.

She turns over, frightened all of a sudden. The voice from the next room continues to drone.

"How will I manage?" May says in the dark, sleep, like warm limbs, bearing her up.

IN THE SMALL flat he owns above the Blue Parrot, Walter puts on a record and smokes by the window.

It is true that the nightclub is failing, that it has, in fact, been failing for years, a slow death the inevitability of which has been so total as to have escaped notice till now. Lately, small and simple expenses—renewals of licenses, lights for the stage—have presented an unaccountable burden. He has never been adept with the books—in school he always did poorly in maths—but in the past they have balanced nearly enough.

The band, above all, is sinking the place. There is simply no audience left for the music. Once, the Blue Parrot was a closely held secret: the stiff pours, the singer's ethereal tone. Touring bands would come and play after hours, having sold out the large concert hall in the city. Briefly then, emerging from the dark years of war, tourists had flocked to places like Glass. The coastline had boomed with factory work. There had been a black and white middle class in those days.

Now paint peels from the window and door frames; in winter the radiator smells of leaked fuel. Piles of records line the walls and the corners: ragtime, big band, bebop, and blues. His phonograph is of the old-fashioned kind, its large brass speaker like a bell, or a flower. It is one of many aged things in the flat, Walter being keen on antiques as well. Never, even when there was money to spare, did he feel in any need of more space. He spends most of his spare time at the club. Only this morning he was there to wash down the floors, to place liquor orders, to tidy the stage. Monday nights are the loneliest time, because he has not seen her all day and won't see her the next.

The record pops with each revolution, the needle riding an uneven groove. The song is "Do Nothing till You Hear from Me." In 1944 that one was recorded. He recalls an alleyway off Rue Gabrielle in Montmartre where, in spring 1945, he drank white wine with strangers. Paris, then, was not the jewel of his dreams but was ragged and beaten, gripped by a primal and desperate euphoria that could not disguise the weight of its heart. It suited him, wearied as he was himself. He remembers the gypsy guitar on a rooftop, the high hat, the slender woman singing in French.

As light falls, he smokes a third cigarette. There was a time when he allowed himself to imagine that May might one day live in the flat, that she might like to leave the city behind. In Glass they'd have had a quiet existence: drinks on the boardwalk, books on the strand. He imagined her speaking of any old thing, harmonizing with the buskers they passed, softly, for his and her pleasure alone. It would have raised a few eyebrows, he knew, but in his dreams they were safe in their love. That was before Virginia was born, when May was still new at the club.

"A fine place," she said the night she was here. She stood by the window, looking out at the sea. On the boardwalk, the lamps had not yet been extinguished; a man passed beneath one, pushing a pram. He had invited her up for a drink, a casual thing. "Any time, if you'd like." In the weeks since first she'd sung "Stardust," she had taken to stopping by his office each night. Peering in, she would smile, pause for a chat. Still he can hear the welcome creak of the hinges, the tap on the door that was quickly dispensed with, since, by habit, he left it ajar.

On the record, a song ends; another commences. Cootie's horn is like an animal's cry, like a peacock's, which is said to be like a man's.

At the window, that night, he brought her a highball.

"Do you like singing here, Miss Valentine? May?"

He drank, having poured out a measure for himself.

"You must know what I think about you."

Was it she who initiated their touch, or has he only imagined that since? There was surely something in the nearness of her, in her eye, that seemed for all the world like permission. When he thinks back, he tries to dwell in that moment, when the space around them trembled with promise, that moment at the threshold between two different lives, just before she smiled and said why didn't he tell her, just before he felt her lips upon his.

Tomorrow, having nothing to do at the club, he will buy a gift for Virginia's birthday. It isn't easy knowing what to give her at this age. Toys won't do; neither would a ring or a necklace. She has probably grown to be beautiful now and wouldn't know what to make of a gift of that kind from a man who these days is little more than a stranger.

Her stamp book remains on a shelf in his office, the small squares pasted in haphazard rows.

Perhaps a record. It needn't be jazz. She might like rhythm and blues, rock 'n' roll, and he smiles, since that would give them something in common.

WEDNESDAY MORNING A notice arrives: a check to the chamber of commerce has bounced. A telephone call reveals the bank's error, a series of transactions processed out of sequence. The situation otherwise isn't dire, but still there is consternation about it.

"Things all right, chief?" Alvin asks from the bar. It was he who found the notice when he brought in the post.

Walter only mumbles a bit. He is thinking of the gift he bought for Virginia: two records, a secondhand suitcase gramophone.

"Only fair you should warn us if we ought to be looking."

"I've told you, Al. It was a clerical error."

There will be a cake, as there is every year. He will telephone Richter's soon with the order. They'll remember when he tells them the birthday has come. Virginia's favorite: chocolate with apricot jam.

Later, when he knocks at May's dressing room door, she appears in red, stilling the heart in his chest. Her beauty has been undiminished by time, only altered, made more enduring somehow; she looks, to him, very much as she sings, exquisite beneath the weight of her life, though he knows she wouldn't wish to be so in his eyes.

"I'm a half hour late," she says. "Not that it matters. Why rehearse if nobody comes? And, anyway, I hear we might not get paid."

"Are you late?" he says. "I hadn't noticed."

She gives him a look and turns back to the room. She leaves the door open, so he follows her in.

"Honest, I hadn't."

In her chair she sets about with her face, seeming pleased to have spoken so sharply to him. "What do you need then?"

"Just to see if we're on for tomorrow."

"Tomorrow?"

"Virginia's birthday, of course."

Last night, Virginia watched *Hawaii Five-o* while May cleared the meager remains of their supper. Unblinking, she looked at the screen. Agnes would have disapproved of the program; often she disapproved of such things. In all the years they were together, she never came to the club, saying only that it wasn't her kind of music. Last night she'd have said, "Is your homework done, girlie?" and Virginia would have told her the truth. As it was May didn't manage the question, only asked, "What's on at school for this week?"

"I don't know where she'll be from one minute to the next," she says now. "I hope you haven't gone to much trouble. It's kind, but she's not a little girl anymore. She's liable not to show up at all."

"Surely she'll remember," he says.

"I'll ask her. But I can't say it'll help."

"I've got a present for her. And a cake."

"A better gift would be keeping her mother employed."

"It was only a clerical error."

May can scarcely hide her disgust. Lately she has been this way with him, an end to many years of what seemed a détente. It was disgust she felt, also, that night in the flat. Something had changed from the moment it ended. In silence, she gathered her things from the floor, her earrings and bangles, the comb from her hair. She straightened her dress, which, in haste, had not been removed. That is something that has stayed in his mind: the dress not having been fully removed. It fills him with shame, remembering that. With shame and with yearning as well, for he never saw the bare silhouette of her body.

Now she says: "Only don't go to more trouble."

Nine thirty, the band performs "Love Me or Leave Me." She was right: they didn't need to rehearse. They scarcely interact anymore, except when they are performing onstage: a glance or a smile, a holler from Ham, and a chorus is turned around or repeated. It makes Walter think of how whole worlds of meaning can pass between two people, unspoken, or of the wordless way love can be made. The feeling is one of great intimacy: her voice mediates the distance between them. And though at bottom a sadness remains, he isn't really lonely when he listens to May.

"I'M SWEET SIXTEEN," Virginia says in the morning. The house is warm and smells of hot breakfast, which makes her think about Agnes.

"That's right, lady," May says. She puts a plate of scrambled eggs on the table, having woken early to make something special. "Will they do anything for you in school?"

"Sometimes on a girl's birthday she gets covered in sweets. By her friends, like. They put whipped cream in her hair."

In her purple dress, May thinks, she looks young; she has not yet become interested in appearing grown up. Her shoulders are small with sharp bones at the top, a light, copper color that shines in the heat.

"Who ever would do that? What kind of friend?"

"Oh, I don't think they'll do it to me. It's for popular girls. Dancers and them."

Again, May wonders who gives her the pills. Despite her prettiness, she has long been thought strange. As far back as her nursery school there was concern, the way an insect or a bird might distract her attention, or the way she might continue to work on a drawing long after other children lost interest.

"You can come to the club after school if you like," May says. "Mr. Chapman insisted on cake."

Virginia nods, pleased but trying not to let on. She likes the way the band plays "Happy Birthday."

"I understand if you don't want to come. I think he forgets you're not a kid anymore."

"I don't mind," Virginia says. She thinks of Mr. Chapman in line at the baker's. "He's a sad case, isn't he, Ma?"

"Yes," May says, irritated somehow.

He asked only once, when first she was pregnant. Just two words, "Is it . . . ?" to which she said, "No." And though she could tell he didn't believe her, she held firm, and he did not press again.

At the Scat Club, things had been required of her. Mr. Aubrey had expected her at least once a week. Mr. Parr at the Hot House had called her crude names, refusing to look directly into her eyes. She can still see him chewing his long, green cigars: "More slut than Saint Valentine, aren't you, May?"

Mr. Chapman was different: he wasn't unpleasant. He'd loved her from the first lines of "Stardust," he said. When, afterward, she didn't return to his office, he said nothing, only started closing the door. It was that that made possible the subsequent years: the knowledge that the child's father was kind. Still, she didn't want him any nearer her life. She never did, and does not want him still. She can't help but recoil at the thought of his touch: the thin fingers, sweat beading on the edge of his scalp. That feeling has grown worse without Agnes, worse because she might need him again.

"Thanks for breakfast," Virginia says.

And May is gripped with affection, watching her leave.

IN THE BLUE Parrot, Walter fills pink balloons. Without helium, they make a dull picture, blown by the ceiling fans into the corners. Ham arrives early, too, in a black suit and tie. He doesn't own a piano—like the other musicians, he lives in the city, his flat too small for even an upright—so he likes to practice sometimes at the club. He waves to Walter as he pulls out the bench, plays a few chords and stops, looking around.

"Virginia's birthday?" he asks, and Walter says that it is. Ham taps out the traditional song, then plays it as a rollicking New Orleans rag. He knows, of course, as everyone does.

Walter listens as he goes about tidying up. In the dressing room, he puts the gin bottle away. He wants Virginia, when she arrives, to see her mother's place of work as clean and respectable. She has not been to visit since this day last year and in the interim might have grown discerning that way.

At five o'clock, Richter's delivers the cake; Walter sets it on the counter with the gift in the greenroom. Five thirty, May traipses in. "You oughtn't," she says when she sees the balloons. By six, it seems it will be a good night: a few older couples, well dressed, order drinks; a group of students affects a bohemian look. The band plays "Nuages," then "Ain't Misbehavin'," which May slows and phrases as a funeral dirge. Her dark mood of the past weeks hasn't lifted; he is glad that Virginia has not yet arrived. When May sits the next number out, the band launches into "Epistrophy." Hearing them, it occurs to Walter for the first time that perhaps they have not so much adopted May's style as been slowly worn down, depleted of vigor. They play now as if they have been freed of shackles.

In her dressing room, she looks for her bottle of gin.

"Oughtn't we liven things up?" Walter says.

"I think they enjoyed it." She moves objects about on the counter. "You want Doris Day? I'm sure you can find that. Or better yet, a rock 'n' roll band. I've told you, you should."

"It's in the third drawer."

"You hid it?"

"Virginia's coming tonight."

She unscrews the cap but cannot find her glass. She takes a small sip from the bottle.

"I never liked this number," she says.

"Will no one rid me of this Thelonious Monk?"

She smiles, sips longer, replaces the cap.

"I'd better get back on. I'll liven things up. A bit of gin always livens things up."

"Do you think she'll come, May?"

"Virginia?" she says. "Seemed like she would when I saw her this morning. But I told you, I don't know where her head is these days."

Briefly she wants to mention the pills. She is looking at his reflection (how old he has grown!), and she wants to say, "I'm worried about her." That is what she would have done if Agnes were here, and Agnes would have put an arm over her shoulder, said, "Hush, lady. I'll speak to the girl." But the moment passes, and her wanting that fades; she retrieves the bottle again.

"I tried to warn you. Now I've got to go on."

WITH DAY FALLING, Virginia hurries from school, having lingered for a time on the grounds. She will stop in at home, deposit her books, then catch the evening bus into Glass. She takes the new route, avoiding Muldoon, because sometimes she sees Fergie Davidson there.

At school, no pomp attended her birthday. When she was younger, the teachers always remembered. In year four there was a crown that you wore, and you got to decide which games would be played. Her mother considers her too old for such things, too old to eat cake and have a gift from Mr. Chapman. But she looks forward to her party tonight: it is a chance to feel like a child again.

The pill she took at lunchtime has mostly worn off. The edges are returning to things. On the east side, trees do not line the streets as elsewhere in the city they do. Gaining distance from school she traverses Old Pike, a broad street of brick warehouses, empty, abandoned. Here, you'd never know the seaside was near. The air is dusty and eerily still; she dislikes this section of town. She would not have to cross it if she rode on the bus, but lately what little money she has she spends on her lunch or gives to Jeanene.

With Agnes gone, she is often alone. For that reason, too, she is glad of the party. Agnes never came to the club, not approving of the music or drink, but she would wait up and sit with Virginia after, listening while she recounted the night. She has wondered today whether Agnes remembers, if she has marked the occasion, wherever she is. Perhaps there is a picture she's kept: All three of them after they'd been to *Swan Lake*, or standing in front of the secondary school; or the one of only Virginia and Agnes, taken at the seaside in Glass. The sun shining, Virginia holding red Brighton rock, Agnes's head wrapped in a blue and white cloth. In all the photos they took through the years, Agnes never looked at the camera. There was something almost ghostly in that, her presence strong but elusive, unfixed. As if she wished her face would be forgotten, as in truth it is beginning to be. If you looked now, you'd long for her large, clumsy teeth, a dark eye, but instead would see only her jaw, the thick cords of her neck as they twisted away.

It is someplace nearby that Jeanene buys the pills. Virginia still has two in her pocket. The man who sells them stands outside a garage. She saw him once, shifting about on his heels. He lives with his mother on Roosevelt Street, something he will tell to anybody who asks. His training shoes were battered and scuffed. Jeanene says he is not the full shilling.

She turns up James and, rounding the corner, finds herself face-to-face with Fergie Davidson, smoking one of his scented cigarettes. He has appeared as if from thin air, his ungainly body leaned up on a wall.

"Little Miss," he says, exhaling smoke. "I never see you walking home anymore."

His hands are broad, indelicate things. Nobody else is about. She mutters something, his name, and tries to keep walking, but he reaches and takes a hold of her dress.

"What's the hurry?" he says. He stamps out his cigarette. "Always rushing. Little Miss A-Level. I see you taking those pills from Jeanene."

"Leave me alone, Fergie," she says. "I've got to get to the club."

His father clears rubbish at the primary school. His mother used to deliver the post but can no longer work because of her leg. Virginia remembers seeing him as a boy, grasping his mother's hand before crossing the street, letting go again as soon as he stepped onto the curb. Father and son didn't speak on the schoolyard. Carelessly, Fergie threw his trash on the ground.

"Jazz club. Right."

He moves his fingers in the air as if keying a horn.

"You could stand to be a few minutes late. Place like that, they'd lose track of the time. I won't keep you long, I promise." He laughs.

"It's my birthday," Virginia says, and then wishes she hadn't.

"Ah, how old? All grown by the look of it. Daddy gonna throw you a party?"

Surely, he has said the same thing before. Often he is on about her mother and Mr. Chapman. A white man would have a taste for that sort of thing, he has said. Owning a jazz club and all. But somehow it is different this time, different because of the birthday, perhaps.

"You know I never had a daddy," she says.

"Don't act stupid, Little Miss A-Level."

"I'm not."

"Who d'you think paid for those shoes?"

She looks down at her black Mary Janes, a gift from her mother for no reason at all. She remembers opening the large paper box, the silver buckles shining on top.

"Who d'you think bought that dress, Lemonade?"

Behind her glasses, her vision has blurred. Fergie smiles, but he doesn't seem to be happy. She feels suddenly very ashamed. She thinks of her mother saying she needn't come to the club, of Agnes saying, "There was wickedness here." Of Fergie, as well, how it's said that he fancies her. The cruel ease of harming a person you love.

Two blocks on she stops running. Fergie has not been following her. In the din of a nearby construction site, she cannot hear the sound of her breath. She is choking; she wipes tears from her nose and her lips. Her hand shaking, she puts the last pills on her tongue.

SHE ENTERS WHILE the band plays "Embraceable You." From the stage, May sees her move past the bar, face obscured by the lights but recognizable still. Normally she would find Mr.

Chapman, sit with him for a number or two, but instead she wanders on in the direction of the greenroom, scarcely lifting her feet from the ground.

Walter sees Virginia as well. She passes very near to his seat, not taking any notice of him or of the balloons. There is a dreaminess to her, a slowness. The last year has indeed seen her a beauty.

The song ends, and amid the applause he stands and follows Virginia. He knocks twice, lightly, on the door to the greenroom, as he does always before he enters her mother's dressing room. She is seated at the far end of the sofa, holding her eyeglasses as if to examine them. She does not look up when he enters the room. On her face remains salt where her tears ran and dried.

"Right, Virginia?" he says.

Now she looks to the door. Her hands, still holding the glasses, have fallen into her lap. He knows that she cannot see him clearly, her vision being abnormal without them.

It is when she looks back down at her glasses that he becomes certain something is wrong. That dreaminess is a barbituric haze. You come to know it through the years in a club. She is motionless, not making a sound. He approaches and puts a hand on her shoulder. "Your birthday," he says, but she doesn't respond.

"You're sixteen. I can hardly believe it. It seems no time ago we used to play jacks."

Still she makes no reply. At the table, it is all he can manage to cut her a small piece of the cake. "It's the kind with the apricot jam," he says. "The kind that was always your favorite."

Sitting beside her now on the sofa, he puts a bit of cake on a fork. She accepts it, chewing with her mouth untidily open.

"It's a Viennese type, Virginia," he says. "They are famous for their sweets in Vienna."

With her tongue she tries to wipe the crumbs from her mouth but succeeds only in pushing them out of reach. He cleans them away for her with a napkin. Then, softly, almost inaudibly, words begin to form on her lips.

"My mother's a liar," she says; her voice is quavering, hoarse. "Did you know my mother's a liar?"

He puts the cake aside, smooths the hair from her face. He has tried not to wonder whether she knows, though of course, at times, he has entertained hope.

"She's a good woman, Virginia. Don't say she's a liar."

"Even Fergie Davidson knew. He isn't kind, but he tells me the truth. People say he likes me, but I'm frightened of him. That's the first boy who has fancied me, ever. He doesn't lie. He tells me the truth."

She looks as if she might begin crying again. How many times has he regarded Virginia, looking for something of himself in her face?

"She said Agnes was my aunt, but that wasn't true. In the end, Agnes wasn't right in the head. She wouldn't have been, to say what she did. A holy fool. She never looked at the camera. Why, do you think? I felt sorry for her. She braided my hair. She was sacked from a pawn shop. Why would Ma say she was my aunt when she wasn't?"

An image: the woman put forth as a sister. Strange that he shouldn't have known. On the bus he once saw her, retrieving Virginia. A hard woman, thin, head wrapped in a cloth.

A voice, Virginia's, from long in the past, a new set of stamps pasted into her book: "My auntie says it's good I collect. She likes to take colored glass from the sea."

Through the years, he has scarcely given thought to this woman, but he mourns her departure now; truly he does.

"Agnes is gone. I don't know where she went."

She has indeed begun to weep now, the tears slipping easily from the corners of her eyes, erasing the salt stains on her cheeks. He places an arm about her thin shoulders and sways there, the way one would do with a child.

"Agnes made fish for dinner. Agnes made soup. Not the full shilling, but I didn't mind."

His embrace is something warming for her. She has never before been held by a man.

"Your mother loved Agnes, Virginia. She did."

"She never tells me the truth. She said I never had a daddy, you know. But Fergie knew. He says don't be stupid, A-Level. But I wasn't being stupid, I swear."

Another melody turns around and resolves; May's voice fades away just before Posey's horn. There is the sound of applause, half-hearted at first, then louder because they have reached intermission.

Virginia is weeping, her face to his collar.

"You do have a father, Virginia," he says.

Through the door of the greenroom, May hears the sobs. "There, there now, Virginia," Mr. Chapman is saying. "You do have a father. You do." It is painful for May, hearing that said; briefly, there rises a dizzying rage. But she is tired; there is also relief. And perhaps he does after all have the right.

The weeping subsides. Walter holds fast to the girl. She is sleeping, or in a similar state, not fitful; her breath is even and slow. She will perhaps have forgotten all this by morning, but even so things will not be the same.

Without having heard her open the door, he discovers that May is standing beside him. She places a hand on his shoulder. For a moment he imagines there is love in the gesture, then as quickly allows the illusion to fade.

"I told the boys to go back on without me," she says. "I saw her come in."

It was only many years after the fact that he was able to see things as May must have done: the door left ajar, the late-night invitation. Only then did he think of all the clubs she had left, the things that might have been done to her there, and know that she would have left the Blue Parrot, too, if it hadn't been for the birth of Virginia. Where he had seen love, she had seen coercion. It is a gift to be allowed this birthday tradition: the cakes and balloons, the extra money for shoes. His was an accidental trespass: harm done without malice but done nonetheless. An ancient crime, without beginning or end; the eviction she imposed was his due. Now she touches him as he comforts the girl. Now she says, "Walter, what on earth will we do?" and he knows that it is not a gesture of love but of a fragile, uncertain forgiveness for which she has had to dredge the depths of her heart.

It is another gift, and one he accepts.

In his arms, he rocks the damaged child they made.

A Romance

※ ※ ※

Beneath the green canvas awning of the chemist on Lynn Street, shaded from a warm July sun, Abigail spoke with the American man. He was telling her about the years he'd spent playing ball. A display in the window was being arranged, diabetic socks having been placed on reduction, but Abigail scarcely took notice. His name, he said, was Archibald Gates. Employed now in the restoration of homes—mending old timber beams and thatched roofs—he had, in another life, been a pitcher, noted for his slow-bending left-handed curve.

"Wrecked my elbow in Scranton. August the fourth." His accent was like you would hear in a film. "Felt a pop, and that was the end of the dream. Finished the inning, though I couldn't say how."

"Brave of you. It must have been a heartbreak."

"It was."

Abigail had never seen a baseball match in her life, did not in fact care for sport of any description, but what the man said impressed her nevertheless. The job would have allowed him to travel. Across the United States and, in winter, abroad.

"My dad was a military man," he explained. "That's how I came to live over there." He lit a cigarette and exhaled. There was a trick he could do with his lighter. "You live nearby?"

"Yes," Abigail said. "I work across the street, at the gown shop."

In the showroom she told her friend Bethany about him. "I've met a man," she said. "From the States. A southpaw. That's a hurler in baseball."

Bethany was busy sorting incoming dresses. She was younger by two years, seventeen, and prettier than Abigail was, blessed with the long waist and modest, round bust that were flattered by the dresses sold in the shop. Sometimes Mrs. Laughlin asked that she wear them—at work, or at night to the Gem and the board-walk. Abigail would have liked to be asked. Now Bethany wore one with an old-fashioned cut, blue with polka dots, her hair done up in tight curls.

"A pitcher," she said. "Baseball? Oh, Abbie. You really ought to find someone plain. I think a girl could do worse than Harold. Athletes are known for philandering, you know."

Abigail rolled her eyes. There was no reason Bethany should say such a thing. No reason to discourage an interest in Archie when she didn't know the first thing about him. Harold from the chemist's was a dullard, and stout.

"He doesn't play ball anymore. He buys lumber for fixing up houses."

"All the same, I think you'd be better off with poor Harold."

"I don't like him. I've told you. Why don't you go with him yourself." She did not say how she'd been buying stockings for work, how she had regarded the stranger for some time before their eyes met, the cool nylon moving across the backs of her fingers, how he'd said she had the look of an actress about her.

"Be nice, Abbie," Bethany said. "Anyway, it isn't me Harold fancies. It's you."

Bethany was the worst kind of pretty girl: either oblivious to her own easy beauty and charm or, worse, pretending to be. In addition to that, she was a bit of a priss. She would never guess some of the things Abigail had done. Nobody would; not her parents, not even Archibald Gates. It would never be suspected, for instance, that she'd once let Clifford Price have a go behind the gymnasium. That would never be dreamed, though she had done it and had not been afraid. There had been no risk of its getting out, because Clifford knew it would not be believed, and anyway he might not have wanted it known. She had been glad of that then but now wished that he had spread the rumor a bit, if only as proof that he wasn't ashamed.

Clifford Price had moved away after school, as others had and as, at the end of summer, Bethany would. Most young people did not stay in Glass.

AT HALF TEN, Tim Garvey entered the chemist's in search
of an ointment to soothe a bad nail. He'd arrived in Glass some
two days before, having bused in from Croft, and Reading before
it. His own vehicle had been abandoned in Colby, its backseat
strewn with chip shop receipts, pamphlets espousing the wisdom
of term life insurance. "Peace of Mind" they said in large letters, a
middle-aged couple holding hands on the front. He intended to
stay no more than three days, after which time a town this small
would take notice.

He scanned the aisle for the ointment he needed: the one in
the yellow tube, because that was the one that had proved helpful
each time the condition recurred. The girl he'd seen yesterday was
not in today, but that was only to have been expected. She was not
what you would have called a good looker. You wouldn't boast or
show pictures to your friends at the pub. But she had the sort of
milky complexion he liked; you could imagine lying next to her
after, your head resting on that big, fleshy bosom, and her letting
you do that, wanting you to.

The baseball bit had been a risk, he reflected; the sort of thing
that might be disproved. You'd be caught out, having no expertise.
A mess then. He would never have said it except that he'd found
himself drawn to the girl. The accent and the false name had been
more considered, thought out and practiced well in advance.
Archie Gates: trustworthy, vaguely exotic. In the next town he
would be somebody else.

At home, he would not yet be missed. Head office was mostly
indifferent; his friends at the pub knew he traveled for work. His
mother might fret when he failed to ring Sunday, though even

that he sometimes forgot, or skipped doing, not having the heart. Just as likely it would be the discovery of his car that first brought his departure to light. The police department would contact his mother. Perhaps they would contact Lorna as well. "What are you telling me for?" she would say.

A young man stood in back of the counter. "All right?" he said while Tim counted his money. "Nice day out."

"Summer's come," Tim agreed. "Say, you wouldn't happen to know—" But he stopped short, thinking it might raise alarm, a stranger in town asking after a girl.

BETHANY WAS ON again about Harold.

"He *likes* you, Abbie. What's the harm in a date? It would be fun. You could borrow a dress from the shop."

"I couldn't do that. Mrs. L wouldn't allow it."

"Of course she would," Bethany said. "She lets me wear them out all the time."

Abigail found that irksome and would have liked to say so, but they fell silent because they could see through the window that Harold was passing on his way back from lunch.

"What's new, H?" Bethany said. She was fond of Harold, sensing him harmless, and perhaps also because he showed only polite interest in her. Even now as they spoke he kept glancing at Abigail, who stood at the back of the shop folding garments and, when she became aware of his gaze, thumbing through catalogs of new summer fashions.

"I'm trying for *Next Edison* now," he said, grinning in his usual way. He always had one scheme or another, mostly to do with appearing on TV. Talent contests had been one obsession, baking competitions another. "Have you seen it? It's one of the best programs out."

He was Abigail's age, had known her in school, and like her he lived at home with his parents. His was the broad, open face of a child: small, dark eyes shallowly set. A bit feebly he stood in the doorway, having eaten only a salad for lunch. He had lately been watching his weight, ordering scanty meals at Hyde Pantry, objecting when Debra tried to sneak him rashers of bacon. "I won't see you starve," she kept saying, her voice low and clotted with cigarette tar. She had known him since he was a boy. Today, he'd eaten half of the bacon, wrapped the rest in his napkin for later.

Abigail watched him at the edge of her vision, thinking what a shame and how like her luck that Harold alone should fancy her over Bethany. She would have preferred it be anyone else. Perhaps Archie Gates would prove another exception. He had liked the look of her right off, he'd said. "The look of an actress" were the words he had used, and she'd wanted to ask him which one he meant but knew that that would have made her seem vain.

"Of course, I would think so," Harold was saying. "Being an inventor myself. Not everyone can see how their minds work. But I can. I'd say they're interesting folk."

"It's a good idea, Harold," Bethany said. "My dad would buy it. Abbie, wouldn't your parents buy something like that, for keeping all the various wires in order? My dad is always muttering about the wires, tripping over them and things."

"They'd buy anything if it had a good ad on telly," Abigail said, recalling how her mother had asked for nothing more than a particularly absorbent mop for her birthday, and how, when it arrived, her father in his excitement had cleaned the floors for a month, the only times in twenty-five years of marriage he had done so.

"I've got a clever idea for an ad," Harold said. "It looks like the head of Medusa, but instead of snakes there's all different wires and cords." He said this with a smile and a tone of satisfaction, the image being clear and very pleasing to him.

"That is clever, Harold," Bethany said.

Abigail turned the page in her catalog.

"Doing well, Abbie?" Harold presently said, his voiced raised because he hadn't moved from the entrance and she was still at the rear of the shop.

"Well enough," she said. "Bit bored today."

"No offense taken," Bethany said.

"That older bloke, yesterday, wouldn't leave you alone? You'd remember. Had a funny American accent?" He pretended not to know what it was she had bought, though of course he had not forgotten the stockings. Her legs now were obscured by the counter, otherwise he would have looked to see if she had them on. He loved Abigail because there was a sadness about her. He wasn't a proper chemist, hadn't stood for exams, but still he knew about the pills she was given: a sleep aid, something for nerves; you found out about that sort of thing with his job. Harold did not take medication himself but felt it was something they shared nonetheless.

"Archie," she said, looking up for the first time with interest. "That's his name. Archibald Gates. He was a baseball hurler, you know."

"He was back in again. In the chemist's, I mean. Buying creams for a toenail fungus this time."

"That's really hot stuff," Bethany said. She laughed until she was red in the face. "What a dream boat, Abbie. What a catch that Archibald Gates would be."

"Just drop it, you two," Abigail said.

"It was probably only for his granny or someone," Harold put forth, sensing her upset. A kindness, because he knew better, of course.

DAYS PASSED, AND Tim Garvey stayed on in Glass. He saw the girl again when she made change at the bank. She was wearing the stockings he'd seen her select. He had not gone to visit the shop where she worked, having faith that he would come upon her by chance and knowing that it would be better that way. Morning to night he wandered the village, the four blocks at its center, hills to the east, the headlands and boardwalk north by the shore. Meals he took at the Cavalry Inn, charged to a bill that would never be paid.

He could not have said, if asked, what it was about her. He'd have put her at twenty or so, as Lorna had been when first they were married. In those days he'd been a security guard, ill paid and ill fed but deeply in love. Graveyard shifts under shopping mall light, he would sit by himself and think of his wife. She was given to chills and to frightening dreams, so she disliked his being gone through the night. It had seemed for a while at that early juncture that he might have been delivered from hardship. Days, young people would come to the mall. He liked to watch them interact with each other. His own childhood had been spoiled by the loss of his father, who'd fallen to his death from a scaffold. His mother was never the same. The young people he encountered were as yet unblemished. Because nothing bad had happened to them, they seemed to feel certain that nothing ever would. It made him tenderhearted toward them, hopeful that they might not be mistaken.

Sometimes now, when he was worn down with travel, he would find a girl who was on the game and take up for the night. He would buy her coffee, or dinner if she wanted it (some of them didn't), and she would sit with him in the restaurant in full view of the world; later, in his rooms, it was just as if she were a part of his life. They were almost all of them kind. They always understood it was just that he was lonely. He reminded himself that it was different with the new girl, different because she was not on the game.

When she came out of the bank he was waiting for her, slack against a light post, chewing a toothpick. She smiled when she lifted her head. It had been a long time since anyone had been happy to see him.

"I thought that was you went into the bank."

"It was."

"I'd hoped I would see you again."

They walked the block and a half back to Laughlin's Gown Shop. She told him about Bethany, making her out as a bore, overstating her beauty so that it would disappoint him in person.

"You've moved to Glass?" she said.

"Only doing a bit of business. There's cheap birch to be had. But I'll be back; I'll arrange it that way. I've taken a liking to the place."

This seemed to please her.

"A bit quiet, I'd have thought, for someone who has been an athlete."

"I like quiet places," he said. "And quiet people."

"But I guess you've been all over. All the big cities."

"Ah, well the fact is the farm teams mostly play smaller towns. Memphis, Nebraska."

"But you've been in Mexico?"

"Tried a comeback in Japan," he said, thinking of a program he had watched about an ancient kind of archery. He had been taken with the slow manner in which the bows had been drawn. His mother preferred dramatic programs and sitcoms, but she would usually watch something else if he wanted.

"Were you in Tokyo?" she said.

"Yes, and then in the mountains."

In the years after the divorce he had wondered about things: when precisely Lorna had given up on him, when she had got used to sleeping alone. Later, when he began setting out on the road, she had not seemed to mind his absence at all.

It was a pleasure now to walk down the street with the girl, and not only because he knew they were seen. Near the gown shop they paused to finish their chat, and he said he would like to see her again. She smiled, and over her shoulder he was able to catch a glimpse of the friend. It was true she seemed to be a prettier type, but that did not change things about Abbie. She had a bit of weight to her, Abigail did, but it was by no means unpleasant. Even though she was not on the game, you could tell by the way she had of looking at you that it would not have been the first go-round for her. He did not mind that, either. It was all right.

They agreed to meet the following evening.

IN HER DREAMS he was there, always waiting for her. Against another lamppost, reclining, he smoked; in an alley, steam rose from wet pavement.

I'd hoped to see you, he said.

I knew you'd be here.

In clean sheets, and smelling of leather and soap, he was gentle. His hands when they touched her were coarse. He wore no rings; she'd noticed that as soon as she saw him. He was handsome—she had noticed that, too—age having lent him an elegance. He was a man, where Clifford Price was only a boy. They both agreed it didn't matter about his being older.

She woke trembling, the familiar terrain of her bedroom slowly reasserting itself in her mind. A thin sweat had broken out and she threw back the covers. She ran her fingers over the places he'd touched in her dream.

"THERE'S A ROOM where you can try on whatever you like," the lady said in the secondhand shop. He'd been rummaging some time through the racks of old clothes.

It was difficult, always, to find things that fit him, being slender with jangly limbs. It wouldn't do to wear sleeves that came short of the wrist, any more than it would to have grimy stains at his collar. Whatever desperate point his life might have reached, he would have to maintain certain standards. Thus far he had found a brown woolen suit and a shirt checked in pink and pale blue with French cuffs.

Inside his shoes he wiggled his toes. They slipped against each other, slickened with ointment.

He'd left most of his own clothes behind. Not that they were any great shakes themselves, but it would have made things easier not to have had to. It had been necessary that his luggage be found with the car to create the impression of having left it in haste, or else intending to come back. He never carried valuables in his suitcase; if he had, he would have taken them out and strewn the rest of its contents about the trunk and the ground.

In the fitting room he looked at himself in the mirror. It seemed to him that he ought to look older.

Once again, he assured himself he'd done the right thing. He had not wanted to abandon his mother. Only he'd come to the end of his savings. The money from his policy would see her through to the end; she would never be thrown out into the streets, as she might have been if he had not left. He glanced at his wristwatch: a quarter past three. She'd be watching her hospital program. After that would be the one with the judge. She had been in hospital last year herself, but that had not lessened her interest in the program. When he was not on the road he would watch it with her, and sometimes she would take hold of his hand while she filled him in on what he had missed. "These two are having it off," she would say. "About time. They were all lovey-dovey for years. And this one lost a patient last week. Prescribed the wrong dose of something or other. He was distracted because his daughter is pregnant by a negro."

Mr. Jessop would see that the policy paid. There would be red tape, to be sure. It was not the best one on offer, ornamental—to show that he, too, was a client of the firm—but, in a sense, that was all the more reason why it would pay.

He counted the cash in his wallet, surprised to see how little remained. He ought to have left by now, on to the next place, a more distant town where odd jobs might be found. It was all being put into jeopardy. He would have been long gone, if not for the girl. Again he told himself that, though he feared something else: a kind of creeping paralysis, a slow failure of will.

On the clothes hanger he replaced his own tattered shirt; he would wear the pink and blue one out of the shop. He did the same thing with a pair of brown leather oxfords, his own shoes discreetly returned to the rack. The suit was too expensive to buy and too fine to be swapped for without drawing notice, so he returned that as well to where he had found it. Unfortunate, because it was slim fitting and stylish. The shopkeeper had seen him come out of the room, had nodded when he held up the items in his hands, when he shrugged to indicate that they hadn't fit. Now her back was turned and she whispered into the phone, saying that what she was being told beggared belief. He took a chance, a risk he knew he should not have, and let the suit fall from the hanger into his briefcase. It gave him no pleasure at all. But the woman did not turn around, not even when he rapped a good-bye on the counter, not even when the bell sounded his step through the door.

SHE MADE HER way to the place they'd arranged, walking quickly, afraid that he might not be there: half six was what they'd agreed, and the clock on the bank said six forty-two.

All day she had been marking the time, scarcely saying a word in the shop. At home, there had been the usual fuss, her mother clucking like a hen through the kitchen.

"Your father's destroyed my best saucepan," she said.

The air was hazy with smoke.

"High time he opened a tin around here, but didn't he fall asleep with his soup on the stove? Old fool. Lucky thing he didn't burn the place down."

"He's all right then?" Abigail said. She could not help the love she felt for her father. Married once before meeting Abigail's mother, he was, at seventy, as she might have imagined a grand-dad: kind, only vaguely engaged. Sometimes, coming into a room, she would find him daydreaming, caught unawares. "Right, Abigail?" he would say, as if he were startled by her very existence. She liked to think he might once have been different—hand-some, untimid—and that some vestige of that better self might still prove to be latent in her.

"Oh, fine. Out the door before the fire was doused. He'll be down the Green Man for a pint."

Her mother's hands had gripped the edge of the counter.

"As if I won't be widowed soon enough as it is."

Now, along Douglass, her spirits recovered; all thoughts of home simply floated away. Milk bottles chimed in the bed of a truck. Holly blues flitted from flower to bush. He was there, just as he'd said he would be, a kept promise on the library steps. Her whole body might have been a pool of warm liquid into which a stone had been dropped. The brown suit he was wearing flattered his height; she would tell him it did when she got up the courage.

She wore a pink blouse and pale yellow skirt. They were the best bits of clothing she owned; once, when she'd worn them, she'd heard Aubrey Gillingham say, "God's truth, like she's choking on tits."

"Am I late? I couldn't get away from the house. My mum and dad were having a row."

She'd left her mother alone in the kitchen, bent over, frantically scrubbing the pan.

He looked up. Blue sky persisted yet overhead, it being the height of the season. On the steps, all around them, seagulls had gathered. The sun was pleasant on the side of her face.

He'd seemed to smile when she mentioned the row, and she wondered if it amused him that she lived with her parents.

"Not late at all," he said. "Not at all. I'd have waited a good deal longer than this."

She chewed at the nail of her thumb.

"I thought we'd see a film. You like movies, Abbie?"

"I like them, sure."

"There's a film at the Gem."

"Maybe we'd walk a bit first?"

She did not mind being bold in this way. She knew that he would do what she liked, because he was the sort of person who would. With another sort of person—one her own age, for instance—she would have gone to the film without taking a walk. Boys her age couldn't wait for an hour. He would pay for the movie: he was that sort as well.

"Sure. That's a fine idea. Good we should talk. By the sea, maybe? Not so many people around."

They walked west until they reached the marina, through cobbled streets in the old part of town. The sounds there were of boats in the dock, masts whipped by rigging moved in the wind. On the footpaths between small parks they went on. He was relieved she hadn't spoken of dinner and hoped she might have eaten at home.

"You look nice in your sweater," he said.

She looked at his eyes, which seemed to linger over her body, but not indecently, before rising again to meet hers.

"I knew we'd get on as soon as we met."

"I thought it strange at first, your looking at me. I was told to stay away from men who hang about like you were."

"And do you still think it strange?"

"No. Not anymore."

"I'd taken a fancy to you."

On a bench at the crest of a hill, two women were sitting and sharing ice cream. Abigail looked at them, puzzled somehow. They were silhouetted against the sky, backlit by residual glow from the sun, which had a few moments earlier dipped into the sea. In the farther distance someone was flying a kite.

"Come off it," she said.

"You were a sight for sore eyes."

It was far too early in the encounter for crying. She looked away from him because she did not trust herself. It happened this way: somebody would say something kind, and instead of gratitude, she would be overcome with this sadness.

"Was it a laugh for you when I said about living at home? I mean to move out as soon as I can."

He touched her arm at the underside of the wrist. He touched it there and lifted it, so that her forearm fell along the length of his own.

"Not a laugh," he said. "No, not at all. When I'm home I take care of my mother, in fact. I've had to since my old dad died in a fall."

It was the first bit of truth he had spoken to her, and with it the accent he'd been affecting began to fall away and diminish. She did not seem to take any notice, but in his own ear it sounded alien, strange.

"My dad's old," she said. "But I like him."

"I'll bet he's nice."

"I'll be moved out any time now," she said.

"Do you like it, working in the gown shop, Abbie?"

"Not very much. Mrs. L favors Bethany as a matter of fact. Anyone would. Well, you saw her, I guess."

"She doesn't measure to you."

"Stop it," she said, really wanting him to.

"Is your skirt from the shop? It suits you," he said.

She pulled her arm away, not completely but a little, so that her hand rested nearer his elbow. She knew he would understand from the gesture that she'd prefer to talk about anything else.

"When you've moved out will you go away from here, Abbie?"

"I'd like to."

"Is there a dream you've got? You could do anything you wanted, I'll bet."

She blushed. "When I was little I wanted to be a veterinarian. For horses and things. But I don't really want to be one anymore. Now I only want a chance to travel, like you've got."

"You get to where you're missing a home."

It was becoming difficult to see on the path. In the distance their view opened onto the sea, which was opalescent in the last of the light. The beach itself was visible only where it had been washed with the water, and there it was opalescent as well. A dog was fetching a stick in the surf.

"I don't think I would miss it," she said.

They turned around and this time when they walked past the bench the two women who had earlier been there were gone.

"We could sit a while." A breeze had sharpened, and she moved so that she was closer to him.

"You've given up on a film?" He wondered if she was feeling afraid. For his part, he was, inexplicably so. It was as if, with the one true statement about the death of his father, he had pulled a single stone from the base of a tower. All the many lies he had told, most of all the ones he had told to himself, fell and clattered, an empty ruin inside him.

"The cinema's where the kids go to be alone. We could find someplace a bit quieter, Archie."

She had led him to the bench, and they sat in the dark.

"It's quiet in the cinema," he said.

"I'm not a child. It wouldn't be my first time."

She was kissing his neck. Her mouth was warm and searching. He was accustomed to the expert movements of whores with whom he spent nights in unfamiliar cities; now his heart was breaking for her, the desperate and curious way that she kissed him, her mouth opening and closing like something just born.

"My name is Tim Garvey," he said, the voice and the accent now wholly his own.

He felt her pause almost imperceptibly, a single tremor, a single missed beat of the heart. Then she pressed herself further against him and brushed a lock of hair from his face.

"I've run away from my life."

She was on top of him. Their faces were touching, but she would not open her eyes.

"Abbie, I never played ball. I'm a salesman."

"Please stop it," she said. "I wish you would stop."

He put his arms, which had hung at his sides, around her. He held her there, arrested, her chin on his shoulder. Her body was plump, but he could sense it was fragile. Her breath seemed to rattle the cage of her ribs. Lorna had been like that when afraid in the night.

After the fall, his father lived seventeen days. He had not woken up. In bed he'd lain all the time without moving, a bur-bling sound escaping his lips. His mother, having no place else to go, had spent those last nights in bed with Tim.

Her breath, too, had been rather like this.

FROM THE BUS stop in Colby he walked to his car. In an unpaved lot near the roadway it sat, canted where one of its tires was low. It seemed absurd now. The whole plan seemed absurd: the bags left behind, the checking account emptied and the cards thrown away. An absurdity, too, falling in love with the girl, but even before that there had been no real hope of success. He simply did not have courage enough; his mother would die poor because of his fear.

He had left almost no fuel in the tank, that being part of the foolish plan, too, but had bought a can and a funnel at the garage in Glass. He poured this in; it took longer than he had expected. In the sun he felt himself terribly wearied.

It had been midnight before they were parted.

In Wexford, he stopped for more fuel and a bite. He ordered soup and a sandwich but didn't eat very much. From a box he telephoned to his mother.

"Where had you got?" she said. "I'd about given up."

He leaned against the glass wall of the box. In the background he could hear the white noise of the TV.

"I've got a mystery on, but it doesn't matter. I already know it's the daughter. Give me two secs, I'll turn off the sound. It's always the one you think couldn't have done it."

He could see her there, leaning forward a bit in her chair. She wore the same pale blue night dress as she had for years. She hardly ever wore anything else. Every Christmas he bought her another to replace what invariably had grown soiled or torn.

"All right, Ma?"

"I'm out of milk. I can't drink my coffee without it."

"I'll be back by the end of the week. We can watch your hospital show."

"Ah, good," she said. "I'll have to tell you about it. There's a lot that's gone on since the last time you saw."

ABIGAIL FOLDED AND refolded the clothes. She had not slept; her eyes were swollen and red. Bethany looked at her from time to time, intently, searching her face.

"It didn't go well, Abbie?" she said at last, because the silence had festered between them.

"It was grand."

"I'm glad. What did you wear? I think you would have looked nice in this." She held up a green muslin frock.

"I wore a skirt and a blouse, as a matter of fact. Not that it's your business and not that it matters. He was more interested in what I had on underneath."

Bethany blushed. "Abbie! I told you to watch out for an athlete. Did he have only one thing on his mind?"

"I had only one thing on mine. He's a grown man, and I'm a grown woman. He wasn't at all like the other boys I've been with. He wasn't at all like Clifford Price, if you wanted to know."

"It's better not to, Abbie," Garvey had said when she pleaded with him to bring her back to his rooms, and again when she suggested they run off together. She did not care that things he had said were untrue, did not care that his life had been perfectly plain. When he told her about the man falling from a scaffold, about how he had died on the seventeenth day, she knew that this time he was telling the truth. That he had lied before only heightened her affection; he had done that because he thought he was not grand enough for her, but in fact she loved him more for not being grand. "It's better we should imagine what it would have been like. You can live a great deal longer on something imagined."

On her lunch break she walked the short block to the chemist. Her strength was coming back by degrees. Harold looked up as she stepped through the door. She ignored him and stood by the tall rack of stockings, touching them with the backs of her hands.

At the counter he asked her how she was faring.

"Fine, Harold," she said. "Everything's fine."

She could not bring herself to look at his face, so full, always, of ludicrous hope.

"I'll have a box of those," she said with a gesture.

She was pointing to the small shelf behind the till. Harold glanced briefly over his shoulder. When he turned back, his expression was blank.

"I'm sorry," he said. "Which ones did you say?"

"In the blue box, Harold. The blue condoms, I said."

He turned again, his whole body this time, and was turned for rather longer than was needed to retrieve them.

Harold knew well what people said about him: that he was simple, that he hadn't been a promising student. It was why he took pride in his job at the chemist, why he dreamed also of a turn on the screen: because each small accomplishment of that kind gave the lie to what talk there had been all his life. In fact, he perceived more than people imagined. He had known at once, for instance, when she walked in today, that things with the pitcher had come to an end. He had known and had been sympathetic; even now he was still sympathetic. While she paid, despite every-thing and beneath all the pain, there remained a vague thrill at the thought of the condoms. That couldn't be helped, though he knew it was shameful, pathetic, to be thrilled by such a small thing.

"Thank you, Harold," Abigail said.

Under a moonless sky they had stopped near her house. Tim said the street she lived on was pretty. Looking up and down it, she supposed he was right. Chestnut trees formed a leafy promenade; old sodium lights caught wisps of a fog that had descended after dark without their having noticed.

"I hope you won't hate me when you look back," he said.

"Oh, you've got it wrong if you think that. Quite wrong."

They were silent a minute more, and then she let go of his hand. She was nearly home, and she turned once more toward him. He had not moved, was framed in the light of a lamp.

"Archie?" she said. "Tim?" She remained at a distance, standing with one leg crossed over the other. "Only I was wondering something. When you said I had the look of an actress, was it one in particular you had in mind? Only I was wondering that."

"You've got a look to beat them all," he had said.

Outside, she took the condoms from the bag she'd been given and threw the brown paper into the rubbish. Tim Garvey would be on the road again now. The condoms were of no use at all. When she reached the gown shop she would put them on the counter for Bethany to see, perhaps afterward she would take them home for her mother to see also. But in the end they, too, would be consigned to the rubbish.

In later years there would be fondness in the memory of youth's urgency, gratitude for a passion, however short-lived. For now, though, as she walked about Glass, there was nothing of that, only bitter, premature resignation. Beneath the awning of Hyde Pantry, Debra sat smoking; at the Gem, the marquee's red letters announced the film he had spoken of going to see. The vision in which she was married to Harold, having first visited her in the night, seemed more plausible now than finer things ever had. What was easy for others was not easy for her. She moved in a medium denser than air. Bethany would be at the wedding, a bridesmaid; she would say that a girl could do worse. Mrs. L, present also, would remark on the gown while Abigail's mother complained of the heat; and down the aisle her father would shamble, distracted even as he gave her away.

Harold's ambition would come to nothing, of course, and she envisioned the charade of tender disappointment with which they would meet its failure together. He would be good to her, surely, but hopelessly dull, and she would have to try her best to be good in return. She would not hold against him what he never was and could not be, or the natural impermanence of a summer's romance. She would not speak the name of Archibald Gates or give voice to the dreams in which he remained. There would be between them no cruelty after today's, but the memory of it would surely persist. Regret about that would come later, too, on nights when, lifting her head in the dark, she would find that he'd gone out walking again. "Couldn't sleep," he might say, returning later to bed, and unspeaking she would move herself near, allow the chill of her body to say what was true: that she had, until only moments ago, stood at the window gazing privately out; that while no love had welled in her chest as, at last, his distant figure appeared, it had made nonetheless a welcome sight in approach: slow-moving, blue against the black, rutted road, and beyond it the moon a broken dish on the sea.

What Is Meant to Remain

Ж Ж Ж

On the morning of Alma's examination and cleaning, Kenneth Rivers woke early, restless and tired, aware that he owed her an RSVP. He didn't linger in bed; he showered and dressed, not allowing himself to take extra care. There was to be, in some weeks, an anniversary party, given at her home overlooking the bluffs. Cocktails, hors d'oeuvres, a view of the sea. Again, he thought about it with dread, making toast for his breakfast, lacing his shoes. Outside, morning was slow to emerge, a dense fog laying itself over Glass. Sleepily, the village was stirring; seabirds, unseen, called to each other. He had long ago discarded the invitation, resentful of its presumption and pomp. The gaudiness of it: formal script on the address. Naturally, she'd used her married name, Alma Newhouse. He'd forgotten the precise date of the party, though of course he remembered the wedding itself, as well as the date of his own wedding to Alma and the date they had finalized the divorce.

She had secured the day's first appointment, as she always did and had done since he'd known her: the two years of courtship, ten years of marriage, and, now, seventeen of divorce. They'd agreed to the split one night after dinner, speaking quietly, the television muted in their bedroom, mindful of their daughter sleeping just down the hall. Neither had wept or cast blame on the other. It was only they weren't in love. Later, with the lights turned out in the room and uncertain if she was still awake or not, Kenneth had said, "You'll need a new dentist." They were lying there together in the still, moony night, and Alma had taken some time to respond before saying, unfeelingly, "I don't see why."

THE OFFICE WAS in what had once been a house, semi-detached with a pink-washed facade, a periodontist's next door. At the rear of the building were the office and surgery, gutted and rebuilt in medical fashion, but the reception still resembled a Victorian cottage: dark, exposed wood with wainscoted walls. Thirty years he had worked in that space; every part of it held a memory now.

Ruby arrived just after eight, lurching with exaggerated fatigue. Kenneth was seated at the desk in his office, and she slumped down in the chair opposite him, arms dangling at her sides like a catatonic's. She was the practice's only hygienist; not yet thirty-five, already she'd been with him nearly a decade. Sometimes, passing the surgery door, he'd hear her tell a client, "That's enough out of you!" She liked to flirt with him, always had, a habit that had made him uneasy at first but that now had become a familiar comfort. He knew she never meant anything by it. She was married to a doctor at Mercy, handsome, easy mannered, a man Kenneth liked. Ruby was the same way with him. My Swede-heart, she called him, for his height and blond hair. Ruby's own parents were both from Raipur.

Kenneth asked how her weekend had been.

"Short," she said. "You're bleeding me dry. I told Luke it's high time he got me with child, that's how bad I need a day off. Kenny, I'm telling you, I'm considering bringing a life into this cruel world just to get the maternity leave."

She swiveled back and forth in the chair.

"You get holiday." He held up his hands. "Take a day off, Rube. Take a week if you want."

"I always feel so bad for the temps. They don't know what they're walking into: the old biddies of Glass, the absentminded dentist. No, this job is my own cross to bear." She winked. "A strong cup of coffee would do."

"In most practices the hygienists make the coffee," Kenneth said, but stood anyway.

"This is why I could never leave you," she said.

It was to be expected that he should feel agitation; often he did before Alma's appointments. He felt it even though things had never been unpleasant between them: not before the divorce, and not after it, either. Quarreling wasn't their way. The whole thing, in fact, had been absurd in its ease—amicable, friction-less even—and it was precisely that that now caused the disquiet. Everyone had been so well behaved. He'd sent a gift when Alma remarried; she sent him a basket of fruit every Christmas; for years he'd feigned interest in Rick's legal firm and gladness when Rick appeared at speech days, recitals. Kenneth had never been close to remarriage. At first he tried to date here and there but found that it only made him feel sad. That he had resigned himself to the split did not mean it hadn't been a devastation. He had wanted to say that to Alma, if only to acknowledge the loss, but for so long he had been too polite, and now felt that too many years had gone by.

He brewed the coffee, enough so that he could have a cup, and enough also in case the periodontist, Mel, barged in and helped himself to the dregs. The practices had been conjoined from the start, the two men being friends from their dental school days. In the early years, Mel had made a troublesome habit of knocking after hours at the door from reception and availing himself, under pretense of sociability, of Kenneth's nitrous oxide supply.

Now Kenneth drank the coffee alone in his office, with Ruby whistling and making a clamor among the morning's necessary equipment.

Along the corridor, she called, "It will be nice to see Alma."

He checked the clock; it was just past eight thirty. His wrist-watch—an early present between them—he'd already placed in the drawer of his desk.

When first he had brought Ruby into the practice, Alma had been cold and suspicious. "A bit young, don't you think?" she had said, and it had seemed to him that jealousy of any kind, no matter how unfounded, was a marginal victory. That, of course, had worn off over time, and now Alma was closer to Ruby than he was.

He called back to her, "Oh, is that today?" and heard her laugh, because she knew he was different on these mornings, had learned to sense the changes in his disposition.

ALMA DRIFTED IN ten minutes late, not waiting to be met in reception. She wore large sunglasses, which she did not remove until she was standing in the doorway of Kenneth's office, smiling.

"Hello, darling," she said, the words drawn out as an actress would do. She kissed him once on each cheek, an affect he did not recall from the past. She'd have picked it up on some trip or another, Côte d'Azur, maybe, the vineyards of Marche.

She was nearly sixty, as he was now, too, and though he saw her routinely, every six months, he experienced each time this brief dislocation, as if he'd expected her still to be young. There was elegance, though, in the way she had aged; in her green eyes, her pale throat, beauty remained. Her dark hair was shot through with silvery strands. His own hair had thinned considerably, and he sagged about the midsection, the line of his jaw.

"You look great," he said.

She rolled her eyes. "Neither of us looks great, and you know it."

She had long had this way of upsetting his balance. Early on she had enjoyed making him blush, saying, for instance, after they had agreed to their first dinner date, "Now don't start thinking I'm one way just because I do what I'm told in the dentist's chair." In his office now, Kenneth found himself at a loss, afraid they might fall irreparably into his silence, and was beginning to stammer when Ruby appeared.

The two women embraced.

"How is that gorgeous husband of yours? You know, if you ever get tired of him, I'd be happy to sit for the weekend."

It was a joke Alma had made many times. Ruby laughed and led her by the arm from the room. He could hear them as they moved down the corridor, their voices falling to a conspiratorial whisper.

He waited, clicking at a solitaire game while Ruby started in on the cleaning. With patients he maintained a flow of light conversation, as if their captivity obliged him to do so, and at dinner parties during his marriage he had often found himself speaking at length about his work, or a sporting event, or about some odd piece of nautical esoterica that had caught his fancy in a book or on TV. Still, he had always favored solitude, quiet; those forced bouts of sociability left him exhausted. Alma had found him more than once in the kitchen late at night, unable to sleep, with cards spread across the surface of the table, not wishing to be near even her. In those moments he'd felt guilty of something, but later he came to see how it was: her objection had not been to his silence but to his talk; she had found it embarrassing, dull. Rick spoke less but with a measured authority: "I've got a tooth man in Brill," he had said, when first Kenneth had shaken his hand. He'd smiled, revealing a mild fluorosis. "Only I'll dance with the devil I know."

Since the divorce, he'd taken interest in model airplanes and cars, and lately in small figurines cast of pewter, which he painted with great care at the desk in his spare room. He liked the minute detail in the craftwork, found it not unlike the finer tasks of dentistry: the way the smallest pieces of a model fit into place, the shading required to bring out the pleats in a warrior's garment. Under lamplight he worked with dental forceps and loupes. At times he felt as much passion for models as he did for filling cavities or restoring worn enamel. It was something he hid from the world. When last his daughter, Miranda, had visited Glass, he had hastened to pack all the models away; she might have seen them and found it pathetic, he thought—not so much the hobby itself but the pleasure it gave him, the fulfillment. The fact that it was, really, almost enough.

Down the corridor, he could hear Ruby's voice as she worked, and he waited for Alma's to join it again, which would indicate that her cleaning was done. Then, when at last her voice did emerge, he remained a few minutes more. He listened but couldn't make out what was said.

Approaching, he found Alma upright, laughing, it seemed, at some clever remark. When she saw Kenneth she said, "Well, don't just stand there, Doctor."

He smiled and lifted his hands from his pockets; he adjusted the tilt of the chair. Ruby was removing her gloves near the sink, and he busied himself with old X-rays and charts, all of which he remembered by heart.

"And by the way," Alma continued, "you still haven't RSVP'd. Don't think for a moment you've gone undetected."

"Kenneth!" Ruby wheeled round to face him. "We got those invitations ages ago."

He shrugged. "I'm not any good with the mail."

"Some things never change," Alma said.

"He's impossible."

"Miranda will be there. With Patrick. Do not tell me you have other plans."

"I'll be there." His voice emerged with some force. He knew they were only being playful with him, but nonetheless he felt bullied. Women had a way of ganging up on a man.

Ruby held up her hands and slipped out. He pulled on his gloves and his mask.

"Of course I'll be there," he said again. "I would have thought that went without saying."

He swung the lamp into place over her open mouth, prodding the craggy surface of a molar. They'd been together only ten years, twelve if you counted the dating and courtship. Mostly they had been happy, he thought, and when he looked back now on those years they seemed to him much longer than the seventeen that had followed. How many times had she been in this chair? How many times had he traced this terrain? She'd been frightened of seeing a dentist at first, and he recalled her gripping the sleeve of his lab coat, not letting go until he'd finished the exam.

The probe slipped along a graded premolar cusp.

"Alma." He paused and pulled down the mask. "You're still grinding. What happened to the guard I prescribed?"

The tool was still resting on the side of her tooth. She made a few unintelligible sounds.

"Have you worn it even once? You haven't. I know."

She shook her head very slightly in protest.

"Well, don't think you've gone undetected." He sighed. "You used to be such a good patient."

At the window, the day's early fog was retreating, discrete shafts of light emerging red and refracted. Her mouth, at a glance, was as it had been—the filling in twenty, the crown on eighteen—but the slow degradation of matter upset him. When all else has vanished or faded away, the teeth are what is meant to remain. Sometimes, lying awake in the night, when his solitude seemed so complete and profound as to cast doubt upon his very existence, he would walk himself through this familiar landscape and think, *Here is proof. Here witness is borne.*

He prodded further, scarcely attending.

"I really don't understand. You keep coming in, twice every year. Is it only to show me how little you care?"

He returned his instruments to the tray. Sweat pricked the back of his collar, his throat. He held Alma's X-rays again to the light, shook the film like a damning exhibit at trial.

"This is from six months ago, and already it shows erosion. You can't see it, but I can. It's only worse now."

He pointed at the offending gray slides, where the pale stalks of teeth arose blunt and diminished. Her neglect of them seemed a desecration to him.

"Well?"

She turned, a hand held to her face, and spat into the bowl at her side.

"You get crueler every time I visit," she said.

"And you get more negligent."

Already his anger was ebbing; in its aftermath shame and exposure remained. Among other things, he'd been unprofessional with her.

"I'll do what's required here, Alma," he said. "But I'll not be the one who fits you for dentures."

"So what am I in for?"

"Come in for a sealant. And you'll have to start using the guard. You want to wait until after your party? That's fine. Fifteen years, he can stand to see you in a mouth guard."

"The party. So you're coming?"

He said nothing, which she seemed, this time, to take as assent. She had removed the paper bib from her chest, was straightening her cream-colored blouse, her silk scarf.

"Are you doing all right, Kenneth?" she asked. "I'd love it if you brought a date to the party. Ruby says patients still ask about you."

She must have known he didn't date anymore. Early on he had lied about that, but now he had brushed the questions off for so long that the truth would have had to be clear. He wondered, then, if she asked out of kindness or cruelty.

"No more patients," he said. "I learned that lesson when you stopped flossing."

She swung her legs over the side of the chair.

"Listen, are you sure you want me to come? Don't you think it would be a bit strange?"

"Why? Because you're my dentist?"

"Because I'm your ex-husband," he said.

Her apparent amusement was painful to him. "That was a long time ago," she said. "It would be strange if you *didn't* come. Don't you want to meet Patrick?"

Miranda was twenty-seven years old, a schoolteacher, though his image of her had remained somehow suspended in girlhood.

After the divorce she'd lived mostly with Alma, a space opening slowly between them, untraversable not so much for its breadth but for the haze of guilt and diffidence that suffused it. Over the telephone and every other weekend, he had been told of first dates, A-level exams, details of rows had with Alma and Rick. Alone he'd fretted over signs of eating disorder, as later he'd been relieved to see them abate. It hadn't ever reached the point of estrangement. In some sense, he'd been the favored parent, in fact, but he knew that it was only because they had never been close enough to harm one another. She had spoken of Patrick at length on the phone, but all Kenneth could remember for certain was that he was older than she—thirty-five—an attorney, like Rick, at a firm in the city. Now, picturing them at the party, he was unprepared for his own resentment. How could he bear it, people remarking: mother and daughter, each so lucky and adored?

"Of course I want to meet him," he said. "Only shouldn't we all get together some time? In private?" *Just the four of us,* he wanted to say.

"Oh, we'll do that, too," Alma said. "But you know how it is to make the schedules work. And, anyway, this will be fun. You've already said you'll be coming, and I intend to hold you to that."

"Of course I'll come," he said, a third time.

RUBY TOOK HER time arranging the follow-up, and Kenneth spent it alone in his office, feeling that on the subject of the anniversary party, everything had been decided without him. He looked about the room at his diplomas and licenses, the photographs in small frames on his desk; he so rarely noticed them anymore. The acoustic tiles of the ceiling were still dimpled and scuffed from the days when he and Mel had flung pencils at them, trying to make them stick overhead.

Alma appeared in the doorway.

"Do you remember how we used to play that game?" he said, pointing. She had liked to hang about in those days, wasting time with him after hours.

"Sure I do."

"I miss it," he said.

She glanced, briefly, over her shoulder, as though she might have thought her name had been spoken.

"Feel free to choose a toy from the chest," Kenneth said.

She gave him a look.

"Take a sugar-free mint?"

She pointed to a bulge in the pocket of her slacks. "I cleaned you out. It's been lovely, as always. See you on the seventeenth, darling."

ALL MORNING, AS other patients arrived, he felt his usual compulsion to speak but found himself disclosing small, private details that he ordinarily would have held back. Performing a root canal on Joe Frank—a retired professor of literature—he told of reading, in secret, the books assigned for Miranda's grammar school courses, listening while she detailed their plots, not minding if she gave away endings or twists (the dissipation of Wickham, the prescience of Starbuck). When Paul Gillett—a teen with third molar impaction—made mention of *The Lord of the Rings*, Kenneth leaped up to retrieve a figurine from his office, a goblin the boy examined with interest. To Mrs. Winfield—a widow he'd known thirty years and whose husband had been a favorite patient as well—he said, "You've got the teeth of a debu- tante, Alice. My ex-wife is a younger woman than you are, and already I see Fixodent in her future."

There was thrill in being so unwontedly open, a manic, unset- tling sense that he had nothing left about which to be guarded. Alma had said, "That was a long time ago," and it was true, though he knew it might never feel that way to him.

He ate lunch in his office, day-old fish and chips, his fingers wiped clean on a torn bit of newsprint. The post had come and he sorted the bills. He replaced the watch on his wrist. Vaguely, his limbs still buzzed with disclosure. "Sure I do," her voice said again. At his sink, he paused to brush his teeth twice and floss them, eyed his own exaggerated grin in the mirror as—he realized now—he so seldom did.

When, some hours later, the last patient left, he was startled, as though waking up from a dream. He could hear Ruby whistling as she wiped down the counters and chair, a tune he felt he recog- nized but couldn't quite place. When she had finished, she came in and sat down, again in the seat opposite his desk, smiling now in a mild, distracted way.

"If you need to take tomorrow off, go ahead," Kenneth said.

She dismissed him with a wave of the hand. "You know better than to listen to me when I'm like that. I'm never myself in the morning."

"Well then, I'll see you tomorrow," Kenneth said, but Ruby made no motion to leave. She stayed seated in front of him, smil- ing, a kindness that made him look briefly away.

At length, she said, softly, "You don't have to go."

He shook his head. "I think I do."

"No. She'd like to see you, but you don't have to go."

"She wants it to be as if nothing happened."

"Something happened," she said. "And it mattered." She splayed her elbows over the desk, leaning forward as though it were hers. "It still matters, Kenny. She knows it does."

Kenneth regarded Ruby in silence: her short black hair, the strength of her aspect. He had known her nearly ten years, had dined at her house, thrown rice at her wedding. What you missed, really, wasn't marriage itself; it was only the knowledge that there was someone.

"Why don't we go together," she said. "I'll be your date. It's the last thing Luke wants to do. All those lawyers, and he doesn't even like shrimp cocktail."

"I'm no good at parties," he said. "You know that. I'll wind up doing the dishes."

"I'll dry. Or better yet: I'll put a rock in the dip. Someone breaks a tooth, we come to the rescue. No socializing, and you go home a hero. How's that?"

"It's a sound proposition," he managed.

"Think about it. You'd still have two weeks to choose an outfit."

He nodded.

"Good. You'll give it some thought. But you've got to promise not to abandon me when we get inside. Luke does that. I hate talking to strangers."

There was a small red windup toy on his desk, a mouthful of teeth Ruby had brought him years ago, when she had just begun in the office. She picked it up now and set it to marching with its white plastic feet across the surface of the desk, chomping noisily as it went.

"See you tomorrow," she said over the grind of toy gears, and slowly she gathered her things.

DAYLIGHT PERSISTED WHEN Kenneth stepped out; he had lingered only a little. The sky above him was pale blue and milky, the iris of an unseeing eye; fog had not yet rolled in off the sea, though it hung, as if waiting, along the horizon. He would walk the short distance home, his car safe in its space at the rear of the practice. The air was full of all the scents of late spring; the evening was like something lost and then found.

At Douglass, Mel was crossing the street, and Kenneth quickened his own pace to catch up.

"Mel," he said. "Do you walk home every day?"

The periodontist had his hands in his pockets, his head tipped back and bathed in the light. With his long hair and round eyeglasses, he was plainly himself: an old burnout made perfectly good.

"Often," he said. "When the weather permits. It's good for you, Kenny."

"It's a beautiful day."

"I'm of quite the same opinion," Mel said. "Speaking in my capacity as a doctor, of course."

An old joke.

They walked together some blocks. Kenneth said, "I was thinking today. About the dinners we used to have in the office."

Mel looked up without recognition.

"You remember. Alma would show up with dinner and three bottles of wine, and we would sit around in the examination chairs or up on the counters. We just couldn't get over owning the place."

"Are you sure I was there for that?"

"Of course. I'm certain. You used to use my scalers as forks and tease Alma with the mirrors, like you were looking up her skirt."

Mel laughed. "I admit, that sounds like something I'd have done."

It was strange that he shouldn't remember. In Kenneth's mind it seemed there had been countless such dinners, but perhaps there had only been two or three. It happened that way with memory now; time warped, the same as it had with Miranda, the same as it had with the years of his marriage.

"I was doing a lot of nitrous in those days," Mel said, still chuckling. "But I know we had fun."

They parted ways, and Kenneth walked on. Gulls passed overhead; something larger, a swan. In gardens along the road, honeybees gathered, humming in bushes of rosemary, bluebeard. Across Birch the old vagrant, Whitaker, passed. One man jump-started another man's car. A pair of boys kicked a ball against a battered garage door. A woman walked an old and timorous dog.

In their respective homes, Alma and Ruby would be preparing to sit down with their husbands to dinner. Miranda would perhaps already have finished hers. He would eat his meal alone at his crafts table, surrounded by his models, as he did every night, a practice that, by now, could only be counted among the choices he'd made. At the anniversary party he would be the one hovering at the edges of other people's lives, unconnected but by the diminishing pull of memories either shared or disputed. What he had been offered was a place on the periphery, a chance to play at something that was not quite his: like a plain, unmarried girl asked to hold the train of her younger sister's wedding gown, or an infirm boy sent onto the field with a bandage or water for the winger to drink. The thought of such a role had always saddened him, but as he turned for home it seemed that perhaps it would be enough, that he might manage eventually to supplement his solitary pleasures with new vicarious and borrowed ones, as he had come through the years to enjoy hearing stories of his patients' successes and good fortune, to take them, in small measure, for his own.

A Bit of Fun

✕ ✕ ✕

From the main road, heading west with the sun, slowly, Gerald Malden withdrew. Beyond him, a narrow country lane twisted south, descending as it drew nearer the coast. It was a long way for an afternoon's entertainment—two hours' drive in either direction—but the mid-August weather was fine and in the end he couldn't see any harm. There was a cinema called the Princess he fancied a look at, an old fashioned one he knew was still there. He knew because he had looked it up on the web. The facade had been painted, the marquee restored. He remembered the titles of movies displayed: *Date with Disaster, The Imperfect Crime.*

The buildings were brick and cob, near to the road; on one an ad was painted over the whitewash—Fulton's Sweet Cream—letters chipping away. He recognized everything, the advertisement, too. He recognized the trees, chestnut and birch, and the soft, verdant weeds that followed a rain.

Seeing the photographs on the web, he'd been gripped at once with the need to return. It surprised him, rather: the intensity of it. Nearly sixty years it had been. Tickets had cost half a crown in those days. A sixpence for crisps, and soft drink as well.

There would be plenty of time to see a picture, he thought. It was midafternoon; he had nowhere to be. Peter had rung Sunday morning again, a routine that seemed subtly to forbid further contact. Leslie's youngest had been down with the croup but was better now. They had their own lives.

"My husband isn't any good to me, Gerald."

The words, spoken in a whisper, returned. In his small car, nearing the theater, they did. A summer night when she said them, with autumn approaching.

He had been working for his father's delivery firm, driving an ancient Morris Z into town, fruit for the greengrocer, cloth for the gown shop, sometimes even whiskey brought to the pub. Sixteen, he would spend his summer that way. "You'll know a day's work by autumn," his father had said.

He let the window down, turning the knob, taking in the salt dampness of air from the sea. He and Elsie had sometimes visited Glass, even after his mother and father were gone. With the children they'd picnicked overlooking the pier; at the adventure playground Peter had got a splinter and cried. Already then, the flower shop had become a café.

The Princess wasn't really in Glass. There was a different picture house there, called the Gem. The Princess was some miles away in a repurposed barn beside the Payne Road. A novelty now in its resurrection, it had once been a gathering place for the residents of smaller villages and farms in the days when Glass was considered too far. They'd arrived on bicycles, on foot, or in cars. Beneath the marquee, they'd stood and chatted or smoked, men and women who had saved for an evening of pleasure. You wore a suit to the pictures back then; ladies wore dresses, false jewels in their hair.

All of this Malden recalled, and his own suit: heavy tweed too warm for the season. "Handsome," Mrs. Trilby had said.

You couldn't miss the cinema, so alien on the hillside. With its new paint it was almost the same. The marquee was said to come from a Hollywood theater, art deco, not matching the plain stone facade. He could see that it had indeed been restored, its steel lines brightly catching the sun. In a small lot beside it other cars had been parked.

Ribbons he'd brought her, and paper and string. The flowers came daily on a separate truck. "A new boy," she said the first day he arrived. "What have you brought me? What treasures? What gifts?"

"Ribbon," he said.

"Yes, but what sort?" She laughed aloud. In the next months he would learn to discern all the types: taffeta, grosgrain, jacquard, and chiffon.

She had red hair; auburn, she called it. At work she wore it up in a bun. Her eyes were green but with a darkness about them, serenely set. She wore summer dresses.

At the Princess, when they went there together, she would never allow him to smoke. "It will age you," she'd say, "the way it's done me." There wasn't any point in contradicting her claim, though she could not have been much beyond twenty-five. She would kiss his forehead or his cheek when she said it and then drag slowly on her thin cigarette, exhaling a narrow white line, like a ribbon.

The film on today was *And Then There Was One*, a B picture.

"One senior," he said, the money passed through a gap in the box-office glass, as it had been, too, in earlier days.

"Two adults" was what she'd always said then, glancing to catch the flush in his cheeks.

Trilby's was the name of the shop, a single window between the bank and the butcher. When he stepped through the door a bell was set ringing, and she would look up to see him, pretty and alarmed. Above the flowers and the branches of willow and birch, fairy lights were haphazardly strung. She might equally have called the business Loraine's, but she said she had never been fond of her name.

After a week there was something almost daily for her, small orders: jute twine, a bag of glass beads.

"Bring mine last," she had said. "There's never a hurry. Then you can stay for a while and chat."

He paid for his ticket and was given a stub. The doors were old-fashioned, deco as well: wide swinging glass with piping around.

"I have always liked flowers," she said. "Ever since I was a girl. I suppose I have a fondness for beautiful things."

They were seated in the small space behind the counter, at opposite ends of a sofa. The day's delivery had been signed for and put away. She liked to sit there and invited him, too. The wireless played at low volume. She said she was wild about Patti Page. Her hands were busy, always turning small objects; you'd want a cigarette near the end of the day, but the smoke would spoil the flowers, she said. She talked of anything that came to her mind, and he listened, liking her to. He sipped the lemonade she had given him: fresh squeezed from a tree grown in a pot.

"They'll cheer you, I find. When you're in need of cheering. Don't you think so? Do you like beautiful things?"

He did not have the courage to say, *I like you*. He said, "I like books. *Treasure Island* and those."

"It keeps me busy, owning the shop. We can't have children, as it turns out. I haven't told anybody before, but I felt I could tell you. I felt you were kind. It's the reason Mr. Trilby bought me the shop."

"I'm sorry," he said. He could not imagine why she should have chosen him to confide in. It made him feel special, and burdened as well. He looked at all the many bunches of flowers, arranged in pails along the walls of the room.

"That's a disappointment in a woman's life, Gerald."

"Yes."

She was glum all that day. She carried pain, he thought, the way an animal might: calmly, her body protecting itself, as if the deep, silent ache were precious to her.

Other days she was playful with him.

"Do you like music?" she said.

She adjusted the knob on the wireless set.

"I played the trombone for a while in school."

"Not dance music? Have you danced with a girl?"

He said he had, but she laughed, catching his lie.

"It was a lucky thing, the first day you came in. I said it myself: I'm lucky with this one. He'll be a friend. I could tell."

When he was late getting home, his father grumbled about it.

"They want to talk," he said in defense. "Some of them you can't get away."

"You've got work to do, boy," his father replied, not looking up from the crates he was sorting. It didn't really matter, he knew. A plate had been set aside for his dinner.

Evenings, he imagined where she might be. Closing up, the door to the shop locked behind her, sign turned in the window, Sorry, We're Closed. He imagined her cooking dinner at home, a small kitchen, wallpaper patterned with bees. There was the garden with the lemon tree in a pot. Over dinner she would tell about the flowers she'd sold, and Mr. Trilby would say he was tired from work. Business she'd said was her husband's profession. He wondered, would they talk about the lack of a child? It might be that that was something they didn't discuss.

In the grand foyer of the Princess, the carpets were new, a blue where before they were purple or red. He bought Milk Duds because the film hadn't begun. They tasted of the paper box they were in, but he ate them anyway, the sweetness being welcome just then. Elsie had never cared much for sweets. She preferred a bit of cheese at the end of a meal, a cup of coffee sometimes if it wasn't past ten.

The foyer was a long room, like a corridor, high and open up to the rafters. The walls were covered with old posters from films. A few young people milled about and sipped beers, beer being sold now with the other concessions.

"See we don't have to carry you out again, Freddie," one of the youths said, nudging his friend. "You remember last week? All right, what was the film?"

High on the walls, signs made to resemble the marquee pointed the way to the theater, the lounge. The toilets were at opposite ends of the hall; where before they'd been marked merely Ladies and Gents, now they said Femmes Fatales and Private Dicks.

He found a seat near the back of the theater, which was where he had always sat in the past. It was a large room, still oddly resembling a barn; a false ceiling sloped down to salvage acoustics. The screen was very large, and there were not many seats; half were empty, half taken up with couples and friends. When the lights dimmed, he placed his hands on his knees. The projector lit a stream of dust in the air.

She had died, Elsie had, on the third day of March. Winter hadn't yet broken. Since then, he'd moved through the house in a dream, meals taken and as quickly forgotten, the garden half-heartedly raised. You got used to a person, in addition to love, used to the way they acted and spoke, to the sound of their laughter from the next room when something funny occurred on TV. For years she had taught piano lessons at home; now the instrument sat unused and ill tuned. At night in bed, she had liked to sleep very near, an arm or a leg draped over his person. "So you won't float away," she had said. "So you won't float up and out the window from me."

In the film, a policeman suspected a fraud. He said, "There's a dame at the bottom of this."

When Peter had got a splinter at the playground in Glass, it was Gerald who had had to remove it. There was pain, sometimes, removing a splinter, and Elsie couldn't bear to cause pain.

He looked down at the sweets and back at the screen. Widowerhood had so far been this way: you thought a memory might bring some comfort, then found that it caused only guilt or regret.

The curtains were different now, too, he had noticed. Purple velvet, where the old ones had been patterned in gold. He remembered Mrs. Trilby pointing to them, touching his arm with the bare skin of her own. "They're jacquard, you see, Gerald. You recognize that? Same as the ribbons you brought me today."

What a thrill it had been to hear her say it like that: *the ribbons you brought me today.*

Perhaps things would be different if he hadn't retired. If his mind weren't free to run any which way. He might have stayed on after selling the tearoom; one or two days a week would have done.

On the morning of Elsie's death he had thought to himself, *It is happening. It is actually here.* For years, the thought of their separation had been merely abstract; time had seemed renewable then. You didn't know the end of something until it arrived. It was the same way when his mother and father had died, his sister,

Janet, too: as if he hadn't quite believed in the permanence of it. That night, while people spoke to fill in the silence, he had merely looked down at his hands, thinking the world had only one secret left to reveal.

"Would you want to see a picture with me, Gerald?" she'd said. She spoke as shyly as if she were the child. It was July, a gray day, not warm for the season, so she'd made them tea in beautiful china. The flowers painted on were magnolia kobus. You'd know them by the thin white petals, she'd said.

"In the evening? I don't think I could."

"It would only be a bit of fun for us, Gerald. Mr. Trilby doesn't care for the pictures. It would be a relief to him if you went."

There was varnish on her nails he had noticed. She wore lipstick, which matched the red of her dress.

"They'd have an adventure film. I wouldn't mind that. They might have a pirate adventure," she said.

On the wireless, a program was ending. She turned the knob to shut it off and they were left in the silence. She smiled.

"I'm lonely as a matter of fact. That's the truth of it." She glanced out the window. "Mr. Trilby isn't home very much."

He said maybe he could come into town on his bike. His mother and father would allow that if he wasn't too late.

"It isn't the Gem I had in mind," she said. "Only there'd be talk if we went to the Gem. People are so cruel about that. Always looking to take the wrong end of the stick."

He felt himself blush deeply at the suggestion.

"Not Mr. Trilby, of course. He would know it was only a bit of fun. I wouldn't care what people thought, either, only it might not be good for the shop. People wouldn't like to buy flowers from a woman if they thought badly of her. There's a different picture house called the Princess. Two or three miles along the Payne Road. It's more private. If you could manage. If you came into town we could go in my car."

The bell sounded and she put down her cup. A man asked about making up a bouquet. Gerald watched her move about, choosing the flowers: red and purple stocks, lily grasses, and ferns. She had told him the names and he had remembered. The same as had happened with the ribbons he brought.

He wondered how it would be, sitting beside her in a cinema, how it would be with the lights going down. Watching a picture and knowing all the time she was there, breathing and blinking only inches away. She gave cheek to the man who was buying the flowers, asked him what he'd done to wind up in the doghouse. A smile, a wink; they liked that, she'd said.

In his mind, he said, *I am falling in love.*

HE LEFT BEFORE the end of the film, being homesick in the dark and ill from the sweets. Outside, he shielded his eyes from the brightness. It wasn't really much of a film; there had indeed been a dame at the bottom of things.

He had nowhere to go; the thought returned with its usual weight. He would drive into Glass since it was close and since, he knew, that was part of his plan all along. He would look in on the old town: the pub where he'd unloaded whiskey and beer, the butcher, and the bank. Perhaps he would drive himself into the hills.

In truth, there was some anger he felt. That it should have been he who took the splinter from Peter's palm, he who performed all such duties through the years: applying iodine or alcohol to skinned knees, meting out punishment when punishment was needed. Perhaps that was why Peter called only on Sunday, Leslie only when something was wrong. It was shameful to envy Elsie the love of her children, but there it was.

On the evening of their first trip to the Princess, he stowed his bike around the back of the shop. He had not told his parents it was Mrs. Trilby he'd be seeing, thinking they might object if they knew. "Is it a girl, Jerry?" his mother had asked, and he had blushed and said no, it was boys from his school.

"It's great you came, Gerald," she said when he arrived. "We're going to have a good time, you and me."

She drove them in her pale blue baby Austin, all the time describing films she'd seen as a girl. She'd been keen on the cinema then; her town had had a great big one, she said. Her favorite was *Mandrake the Magician*; she never missed that particular one. She glanced at him from time to time as she talked, swerving a bit on the road when she did.

She was dressed as she had been for work, her makeup reapplied, a hint of perfume. She said he looked good in his suit. "You look very handsome," she said.

When the film was over, she didn't want to go home. In the coming weeks, he would find this was always the case.

"How about a walk?" she said. "Or ice cream. Would you want to have an ice cream tonight? I know about a place where we wouldn't be known."

He looked at his watch. His sister, Janet, home from secretarial college, had sulked: "I never had the freedoms he does." She had been the more troublesome teen, brooding, seeming always in search of something just out of reach. A year ago, late on the night before she left home, she had come into his room. "I'll miss you," she'd whispered from the foot of his bed. "But I've never been happy."

"Or we could pull off the road for a bit. There's places to sit. We could chat for a while."

Each week the scene was repeated. In her dresses she would sometimes catch a chill after dark, and he would offer his coat to drape over her shoulders. She would gaze at the stars or up and down the Payne Road. When the picture was over she couldn't sit still. She couldn't keep from looking about.

"I have to get home, I'm afraid. Another time we can have ice cream," he said.

"All right," she said. "But hold my hand in the car. Would you do that? I'm feeling lonesome tonight."

With the windows down, the sea air was fresh, and their hands touched as they moved through the night. Vaguely, coming into the village, she said Mr. Trilby wasn't at home.

At the flower shop, his bike still leaned against the back door. Dropping him, she said, "It's good of you, Gerald," then drove off before he had made a reply.

They saw seven films together that summer. One every Friday, till August was done.

Now in Glass the lights along the roads had come on. The sky was like the inside of a shell. He passed the pub and thought he might stop for a drink. It had perhaps been a mistake, after all. Perhaps it wasn't right keeping vigil at the Princess, with Elsie only just having died. In the early days of their courtship there had been nights of disclosure, a wine bottle dwindling as they told of past loves. Even then, he had said nothing of the woman from the flower shop; even then he had kept the memory for himself. There had been a heat on those nights as they confessed their virginity, a heat the first time she slept pressed against him. It had felt as if no space existed between them, when in fact, hardly noticing, he was maintaining one. Over time, that he had not told her became a part of what there was, the memory as much privately his as a dream in the moments just after waking.

He stopped briefly outside the Green Man, then reconsidered and continued downtown. Hyde Pantry was the name of the diner. He did not get out of the car, only parked it and looked at the front of the building, the stucco unchanged, though the awning was new. He imagined, as he had more than fifty years prior, Loraine Trilby locking the door. He thought of his bike and of the flowers in the window. Now he could see a man sweeping the floor.

With his mobile phone he rang Peter's house. He was still in the driver's seat of the wagon. The safety belt had not been unclasped.

"Dad?" Peter said. "Hang on a minute."

Gerald heard him move to a quieter space. "I know it isn't Sunday," he said.

"That's all right. You can call any time, you know, Dad. You all right?"

"Fine," Gerald said.

"Good. So what's up?"

"Only I was thinking of your mother a bit."

"Yeah?"

"I wanted to say that."

He leaned his head on the wheel. Perhaps the phone call had been another mistake. It was embarrassing, calling this way. There was a silence, and then Peter said, "I'm sorry, Dad. We should mention her more. I didn't know whether you wanted to talk about it or not."

"I do."

"Okay, well we can. Les and I do, you know. So we can."

"The first time I saw her she was catching a bus. She was the only one waiting, and it almost didn't stop. She stood on her toes and waved to be seen."

Peter made a sound that might have been interest, or grief.

"Do you remember you got a splinter at the playground in Glass?"

"I remember we went there. Ages ago."

"I took it out because your mother couldn't bear to cause pain. That's why I took the splinter out, Peter."

"You were good with that sort of thing. You used to hum a little tune while you did it."

"Of course, your mother was the musical one. Well, I only wanted to tell you."

When he'd rung off, he lifted his head from the wheel and found that the day had come to an end. His view inside the diner was clearer now in the dark, dinner guests sitting down, men and women together.

On their last trip to the Princess, she had tried to be gay. She said sweetly how she wished he didn't have to go back to school. At home, his father had commended him brusquely. The merchants in Glass had been pleased with his work. "Take the Morris tonight," his father had said, not knowing that a car had been used all that summer, driven to a wayside theater by another man's wife.

"That's a first," she had said when he arrived at the shop. "A ride in a delivery van."

She was wearing her most beautiful dress, pale silk with a pattern of lavender flowers, cut to expose the rise of her breast. He had told her once that he thought it was pretty, a boldness in the first days of what had since attained an air of intimacy.

As he guided them along the familiar route, she talked about what a fine summer they'd had.

"You'll visit? You'd say you will?"

He agreed that he would.

The picture was *No Stranger to Crime*, and all through it she held firm to his hand. He scarcely watched, only looked at her face in the dark. Her eyes caught reflected silver light from the screen, and he thought she might have wept, but he couldn't be sure.

When it was over, her high spirits were down. She said little as they walked to the van. It was there, as they headed back into Glass, that she said it. "My husband isn't any good to me, Gerald."

He didn't know what to say. She had spoken little of Mr. Trilby, except of his absence, and he was startled to find the man should be in her thoughts. On the road, the van's headlamps cast a small orb of light: moving pavement, at its edges thin branches and leaves. On some evenings that summer her car and its lights had seemed to enclose the whole of the world.

"He's the reason I can't ever be a mother," she said. She lit a cigarette and blew the smoke out the window. "That's a great disappointment in a woman's life."

She spoke as though very distant from him, subdued as she had been that day in the shop when first she had spoken of her childlessness.

"Perhaps that will change," he said.

She exhaled.

"Perhaps there can be an adoption."

"How can there be? How would I manage? Sometimes I wish he weren't kind to me, Gerald. I wish he would hit me or say something cruel."

She had the rigid self-possession of an ill-humored youth, which, he realized, she must lately have been. She was like his sister when a mood was upon her. Janet, who'd said she had never been happy, though there were times in his memory when he'd have sworn that she had been.

From the shop, she directed him to her house. He had never been there and didn't know where she lived. The street was dark but for a light on her porch. It was a small cottage with a rosebush in front.

He stopped but she didn't want to get out.

"Who will bring me my ribbons and twine? Who will sit and be sweet through a dull afternoon?"

He did not want her to go either. It seemed something precious was passing from his life, or perhaps that it already had.

When he asked which was her favorite of the pictures they'd seen, she said she couldn't remember a one.

Through the front window, he saw that a lamp was switched on, pale and plaintive beside the brighter light from the porch. It caught his attention a moment, and as he regarded the house he noticed a wooden ramp beside the steps to the door. Behind the curtains, a vague figure sat in relief, a low shadow that might have been a chair or small table, except that it seemed to rock slowly in place.

He looked at her, uncomprehending.

"Does somebody live with you and your husband?" he asked.

She shook her head.

"Mrs. Trilby, is your husband unwell?"

"I didn't think he'd be up."

"He isn't well, then?"

"I'm sorry," she said.

He remembered holding her hand in the dark, kisses accepted on the forehead or cheek. He had imagined telling his disbelieving friends back at school but now felt he wouldn't wish them to know. It put a different color to things, the husband having been ill at home all the time.

"It was only a bit of fun, Gerald," she said. "He wanted me to have that. He was glad."

She opened the passenger door.

"It doesn't feel right, Mrs. Trilby," he said.

"It was right. It was a kindness you did."

When she moved, her necklace caught a flicker of light.

All the way home that night he thought about them: what infirmity might have fractured their lives, and by what means they had agreed to press on. The image of Mr. Trilby loomed over it all, and for the time being he could see no way past it. An illness, maybe, or a wound from the war; it was shameful, this thing they had done. He parked the van outside his own house, amid his father's cast-aside pallets and crates, a welcome sight, the whole unlovely mess of them. Soon he would be grown and would leave. This would be the last summer of the kind he had known. On the grass that grew beside the door to the kitchen, he lay down on his back, looking up at the stars.

At some length, he became aware of a presence and turned his head to find that Janet was there. She sat beside him, cross-legged in the darkness. She lit a cigarette, something she'd started at school, and handed it to him for a drag. They were silent a while. He was glad she was there.

"These will be the nights you remember," she said.

BENEATH HIS ILLNESS from the sweets, his fatigue, and his sadness, he felt also vague stirrings of hunger. It crossed his mind to have a meal in the diner, but he didn't have the heart to go in.

Through the years of his marriage the flower shop had been with him. Sometimes scarcely thought of for years, even then it had nevertheless been a presence. He wondered if Peter and Leslie had sensed it, and he thought that, in the wordless way of children, they had. It would have been there whenever they visited Glass, in the silence as they passed the derelict picture house, the diner that had at one time been a florist's. That would have been the reason they seemed withdrawn: he had never been entirely theirs. All along they'd have known that, just as they knew without having to ask that their mother's piano had fallen from tune, or that his thoughts drifted back to dwell in a past to which none of them had ever laid claim.

Elsie would have been aware of it, too, a wife's intuition as strong as a child's. She'd have seen it every time he came in with flowers, elaborate bouquets he'd assembled himself, garnished with lily grasses and ferns. Had she watched him from the window as he moved through the garden? Had she seen how he paused to smell the rind of a lemon, to finger the white petals of magnolia blossoms? Yes, he thought. Yes, she probably had.

He backed the car away from the diner and pulled forward onto the road. In the mirror he watched as the building receded, the same way he had done on his bicycle, evenings, the touch of her hand like a wound on his brow.

That touch remained, as all the rest of it did, though time was beginning to soften its texture. They had been young, he and Loraine, hardly more than children at play, their game one not of seduction but of innocence: a bit of fun in a burdensome life, a lost adolescence briefly restored. A bit of fun need not diminish all that came after, nor need it diminish what had brought it to be. Love had flourished in the dark at the Princess, granted by still a worthier kind. There was beauty in the gift Mr. Trilby had made, though surely its price had been terribly dear.

The years with Elsie had likewise been a gift. The presence of her, the weight in the night. She had known when she said "So you won't float away." It was what she had meant, sensing him truant. She had not remonstrated, being better than he, had only stayed near that he not lose his mooring, that he not find himself as he did now: adrift, a mere ribbon of smoke come apart on the wind.

Housekeeper

✕ ✕ ✕

Autumn and winter were passed by the fire, Louise cross-legged on the soft carpet, reading, Mr. Harris folded into the crook of his armchair, watching television programs with the sound turned off. His hearing wasn't good anymore, and the noises only frustrated him. Louise liked the way he held the TV remote in the palm of his left hand and used the forefinger of his right to press the buttons. She would glance up sometimes from her book to regard him, so much like a child in his old age. In such moments—unspeaking and near— she felt extremely tender toward him.

It was curious that he should enjoy the television so much

without any sound. Sometimes he watched football, which was easy to follow, but at other times he watched news or comedy programs, and he seemed untroubled as to their content. Louise would have liked for him to read. She knew he had read a great deal in his youth, and his shelves were still full of old books: wrinkled spines, yellowing pages. In the early months of her employ he had spoken of them, had teased her good-naturedly about the detective novels and pulp romances she favored, but he had not done that now for some time. He'd shown little interest in such things of late, something that made Louise terribly sad. For hours they would sit in the flickering hearth light, she with her book and he with the remote control in his lap and his hands spread like spiders, or like the oversize feet of certain wild birds, across the upholstered arms of his chair. She watched him even as she read, so that she would often reach the end of a page or a chapter and have to turn back to read it again.

"Do you wish it would snow?"

Wood hissed and popped in the hearth. She had drawn the curtains an hour ago, as the light fell and heavy fog clung to the glass.

He asked her to repeat what she'd said.

"Do you wish it would snow?"

"Yes," Mr. Harris said. "I wish it would."

They both looked at the fire awhile.

"I never saw snow until I was sixteen," Louise said. "Real snow, I mean. I lived near to the seaside as well—with my nan—and it only ever dusted a bit. Then I was taken to live somewhere else, and there was snow all over the place. The first day, a girl pushed me down and I cried. I thought I would be wet and freezing all day. I never knew snow was dry before that."

Mr. Harris laughed.

"I wish it would snow, too," Louise said, turning back to her book. "I wish it would snow us in."

THEY HAD BEEN, in this way, together since August. The arrangement suited her well. In the boardinghouse, she hadn't been liked. "Looney Louise," she'd heard Ann Archer say. "I'd lock my doors with her in the place." Over breakfast one morning she'd circled the ad: HOUSEKEEPER WANTED FOR ELDERLY MAN.

She'd found the house at the north end of Glass, where the roads veered eastward, away from the sea. It stood in a long row of others just like it: short, whitewashed, cinderblock things, like a collection of military barracks. Outside, she gathered herself. Growing up, she'd been painfully shy and unpretty; better that way, Nan had insisted, though she'd often felt it estranged her from things. Even now, she felt that: at thirty years old, her very life hung about her like an ill-fitting garment.

At length, she'd knocked at the wrought-iron screen and was greeted by a middle-aged woman. "Esther," she said. "Mr. Harris's daughter."

From the doorway he could be seen in his chair, bent silently over a large bowl of soup.

"We need someone for a few hours, daily," the woman explained as they entered the house. It appeared as if she had someplace to be. "He can feed himself, bathe himself, that. We only need you to wash up, do the shopping. Make sure he swallows his pills."

"His pills?"

The woman lit a cigarette and exhaled. "The bottles are labeled. Just keep the place up."

And so she'd begun working days in the house, riding in on the predawn bus from the city. Through windows she watched the world be remade, the slow rising color of sky, earth, and sea. It was only weeks before she moved in, having entered one morning to the odor of gas, the oven having been left on, unlit, through the night. "It's good of you," Esther had said. "God, how it all slides to hell in a day."

The old man never seemed to question her presence, even when first she began in the house. He treated her as someone who had always been there, the way a person might treat a neighborhood cat.

He had suffered two strokes already, though his faculties were not very bad. At first, the only clear signs of ill health were a weak lower lip, a vague slur in his speech. Unpleasant, that, Nan would have said, illness so plainly declaring itself. But Louise did not find it so in the least. He took blood thinners and other medicine, mornings, swallowing them deliberately. She would stand beside him as he went through the progression, holding a tea towel under his chin. After he had finished she would retire with the dampened rag, and each would behave as though nothing had happened. Eventually, she knew, age would make further claims, as it would have done, too, with Nan if she'd lived. Louise dreaded all that, and what it would mean, but dreaded still more that he should die.

Her bedroom was spare, with one window. It resembled her childhood room: a chair, a washstand; this one had a mirror. The bed itself was narrow and firm. It must have belonged to Esther at one time, but no trace of her presence remained. Louise hung a saint's image over the dresser, though she didn't know which saint it depicted. There had been no formal religion at Nan's, a gospel of relinquishment only. She'd bought the picture at a jumble sale in the city, liking the gentle look of the face. At the boardinghouse, she had bragged of the move: no more rides on the bus into Glass, no more Mrs. Ashford smoking at table. On the first morning, she made Mr. Harris an egg and watched him put strips of toast in the yolk. "A hot breakfast is the key to long living," he said. His appetite wasn't large, but he took boyish pleasure in eating that way. For her own part, she took pleasure as well; a saint would have a pure soul as well as a body.

There were pictures of Mr. Harris's wife in the house: dancing, walking at the seaside in Glass. There was a large one in the corridor from when she was young, seated in a dress with a collar; each time he passed it he would straighten the frame. Louise liked to stand before it, alone, imagining what sort of perfume she might once have worn, what shade of lipstick. In bed at night, she dreamed of the woman, and of Mr. Harris, charming and young. Libby he'd called her; a beautiful name.

There were doctor's appointments, speech therapy sessions, bills to sort and be certain he paid. She bought food and the like with blank checks he had signed, filled prescriptions at the chemist's in Glass. Her only indulgence was a book here or there, chosen from the rack near the front of the market.

She had grown to be more than a housekeeper. She was devoted as a mother, a wife. It moved her each morning when he tipped back his head to show how he'd swallowed all of his pills. From

time to time he grew irritable, and when she asked what he wanted
for dinner, or if the room was too drafty, he would wave his hand
and dismiss her. She was stern with him in those moments, and it
gave her heart a great thrill to say, "If you don't tell me it will be
tinned meat all week, Mr. Harris."

At the interview, she had scarcely remarked it when Esther said
her checks would arrive through the post, administered by a solicitor's office. Now she was grateful for the arrangement. She would
have felt wretched taking money from him. Like a thief she'd have
felt. Like a swindler, a whore.

IN DECEMBER, SHE sent cards to several old acquaintances
for whom she still had addresses. With one woman she'd worked
in a paper goods shop; with another she had eaten lunch once or
twice after meetings of a talking group they'd been in. She sent a
card also to the boardinghouse girls, again boasting of how well
things had turned out. "I tend house for a wonderfully kind man,"
she wrote. "It is hard work, but I know I am doing a good thing.
He hasn't anybody else, I'm afraid." She wondered what each of
them would think reading this and if they'd remember certain
things about her, the trembling of her voice when she spoke, the
way her lips turned blue in the cold; the boardinghouse ladies
would say, "Well, I never."

She received only one reply, from a woman named Rae whom
she'd known years ago at the girls' home, near the end of her troubles. The other letters, it seemed, had been read and discarded, or
perhaps had never found their way through the post. Nevertheless,
she was pleased. She had once felt something like love for this Rae.

She did not open the letter at once, liking the look of it, the feel. Her friend's handwriting was tilted and fine. The address specified Mr. Harris's house. For a while she carried it in her handbag if she went out, hid it under her pillow when she returned. *I only wish I had your courage*, it might say. *I always felt you were born a much older woman.*

Of course, privately, she had known it wouldn't say that, exactly; when she opened it, finally, some weeks later, it was with an anticipatory sadness. "I am married," it said. "I've a girl and a boy. Things have got much better with me. We were always so sad then, weren't we, dear? And for what? Ah, what children we were. I pity my girl she has still to go through it. It's a wonder, having a child, Louise."

She threw the letter away. With Rae, she had walked the bridge over a roadway and stood with their faces touching the fence, leaning into it, eyes closed, the roar of traffic below, imagining that they might fall any moment, open-armed like high divers or crop dusters, to earth. *What children we were*, Rae had said of that time. It made Louise feel there had been only falsehood between them, that she'd never had a friend in her life, after all.

"What is your favorite book?" she asked Mr. Harris one evening as he watched a football match on TV.

"I don't know that I have a favorite," he said. He paused thoughtfully. "No, I don't think I have one."

Louise longed for him to tell her. She felt lonely all of a sudden.

"Have you read all of these?" She indicated his shelf.

"Oh, I doubt it," he said. "Some of them belonged to Libby, and I never did read them."

"She must have had a good mind for books," Louise said, thinking of the woman's face in the picture. Kind, she imagined. Soft with her touch. Nan had been nothing but sharp tooth and bone. "I haven't really."

She wanted Mr. Harris to say something more—about Libby, or about her own unserious books—but when she looked up she found him engrossed in his match.

THEY BURNED WOOD every night, and soon the stack began to dwindle beside the front door. "We can neither of us chop a new stack," Louise said. She was in the kitchen, washing a pile of dishes that had been collecting in the sink for some days. Mr. Harris was in the next room; he didn't respond. Increasingly, she found herself carrying on one-sided conversation like this, addressing Mr. Harris but speaking as though to the walls of the house. "I'll have to arrange a delivery soon."

The next day she made a telephone call, and the day after that a man arrived in a truck. He was young, but Louise felt he had an old face: dark eyes, whiskers on the line of his jaw. She met him in front of the house. He had his hands in the pockets of a corduroy coat, his shoulders hunched against the cold and the wind.

"I can help you stack the wood," was the first thing she said.

"I'd better not let you, Miss," the man replied. He looked at the ground and then back at Louise. "Only because it's my job."

Being called "Miss" made the color rise to her face. She hurried back into the house. From the window, standing obscured by the curtain, she could see him lifting logs from the bed of his truck. Never had she had a proper affair. There had only been a boy in a youth hostel once, and that had been a furtive thing in the dark. Of all things, Nan could not abide sex: the filth, the stark carnality of it. At thirteen, the start of her first monthly bleeding, she'd been made to drink spoons of vinegar, lemon. You'd wonder how your own mother came to be born. Her knickers had been burned in the grate.

She said to Mr. Harris, "He's handsome, that man."

He teased: "You should go on a date."

Louise said nothing to that, only carried on watching the young man at work. She imagined herself a woman from one of her novels, inviting him in for coffee or tea. She would offer to add a splash of whiskey to his, and they would stand, brought close and warmed by the drink. In her mind, she traced the angles of his face with her fingertips, a boldness he did not turn away. When he reached for her, his hands spanned the cage of her ribs. She imagined him kissing her there in the kitchen, lifting her onto the counter as though she were as light as a seashell.

When the job was finished, Louise paid the man with a check signed in Mr. Harris's earnest, uneven hand. Her voice quavered as she offered to make a hot drink; behind her, she could hear Mr. Harris's laugh.

"I'm afraid I've got another job to get to," he said, again looking at the ground when he spoke.

At the bend in the road his white truck disappeared. She watched, relieved to see him depart, to think that he would never be back.

ONE NIGHT AFTER dinner, reading her book, Louise heard a sound like the grinding of stone.

Mr. Harris sat upright in his chair, twitching gently through the shoulders and hips. She watched him, curious, strangely detached: The television light made his face appear pale, but the cheek nearest her was lit warmly by fire. She noted that odd and haunting effect and the lurching, rhythmic motion of him; he might have been a child asleep in a car, traveling over uneven road.

"Are you all right, Mr. Harris?" she said.

Belatedly, panic took hold. She crawled across the carpet to him, trembling as she came to his side. He wasn't shaking very much anymore. His eyes rolled back and forth in their sockets. She placed her hands on his shoulders, his wrists, gripped him. Slowly, the tension dissolved. He was breathing as though after exertion. Already, the seizure had passed.

"All right now?" she asked.

"I'm frightened," he said. He blinked his watery eyes.

Some days later something similar happened. Over breakfast he put his spoon back on his plate and bit down, bits of egg coming out through his teeth. This time, Louise knew at once what had happened. She touched his face with a cloth.

She knew it wasn't right to keep the episodes secret, but neither could she bring herself to tell anyone. Not even his daughter. It worried her heart. Secrecy was the sort of thing that caused trouble, that made people think she might have hurt Nan. At his appointment the following week, the doctor asked if she had noticed a change. She thought of the timidity that had come over him, how if she asked him a question, he was slow to respond, seeking the words.

She shook her head, cast her eyes at the floor. "His appetite is a bit down, perhaps."

After that, she sat nearer to him in the evenings, and when she looked out the window the glass seemed a border between worlds. She spoke more than ever and asked bolder questions.

"How did your wife die?"

"Libby?" he said.

"Did you have another?" The idea seemed a kind of betrayal.

"I never did."

"How did she die, Mr. Harris?"

He spoke as though just roused from a dream. "Very quietly. She was asleep for many days before it happened."

"Did you love her very much?"

"Oh, yes," Mr. Harris said. "I never loved another woman. Never loved a dog, never loved a car or a boat. Never loved anything but Libby. Libby and the girl. Have you seen her picture in the hallway?" he asked.

Louise had moved very close to his chair, and she rested her chin on the arm of it. The wrinkled skin around his eyes appeared terribly soft. With one forefinger she reached up to touch it.

"Yes," she said, taking the finger away. "I have seen it. She was a beautiful woman."

AT CHRISTMAS, SHE bought a small tree, which she placed on a table in the corner of the living room. She spent afternoons and evenings poring over catalogs, trying to decide what she would buy Mr. Harris. She had saved a good deal of money, but she did not yet have the courage to give him something very dear. One catalog offered wood chess and backgammon boards. She had never learned to play either game, but she smiled imagining herself sitting opposite the old man, her elbows on the table, studying the board as she had seen others do in parks or cafés. Other catalogs offered colognes and neckties, monogrammed wallets and handkerchiefs. In the end, she bought him a model sailing ship inside a glass bottle, a gift without utility but one that she liked and thought suitably dignified for him. It arrived in the post, and she placed it, in its simple brown wrapping, beneath the tree. At Nan's house, gifts had not been exchanged.

When Esther arrived, Christmas morning, Louise hardly recognized her. It was different seeing her now, being used to her face as it was in old photos. They embraced outside on the porch, like sisters; their breath could be seen in the cold.

All over Glass the air smelled of woodsmoke, of fir trees, and also of the dark, brooding sea.

Inside, Esther went to her father. He behaved as though surprised she had come. Louise removed herself to the kitchen and set about arranging a tray: the teapot, three cups and saucers, a plate of the dead fly biscuits he favored. Her gift to Mr. Harris was already on a high shelf; he'd been pleased, almost tearful, in fact. Perhaps Esther would see and remark it. Perhaps she'd be chastened by Louise's generosity.

Their talk filtered in from the next room, halting, as though perhaps they had little to say. Already, it seemed Esther wanted to leave.

Over tea, they talked of their daily routines. "He's known at all the shops," Louise said. "Sometimes they won't let me pay for his things. It's true, isn't it, sir? At Star and at Herville's. The hospital, too. He gives cheek to the nurses. You do."

Later, as she left, Esther took her aside. She said, "He doesn't look good."

Louise felt a sudden heat in her chest. "I know," she said. "I should have rung."

"I want to avoid big changes right now. For his sake and mine. Do you think you can manage?"

"Of course."

They were silent a moment, and then Esther added, with a note of apology, "It's the house I can't give up, you know. The sensible thing would be to move him, of course."

They were standing beside the window, just behind the sofa in the living room. They were near to Mr. Harris, but they knew he would not be able to hear them.

"You grew up here," Louise said.

"I did."

"I grew up in a house with my nan."

"It's not much of a house, actually," Esther said. She glanced around it a moment. "I don't know why I can't give it up."

Louise imagined Esther alone in this room, all the furniture cleared out and sold.

"I think it's lovely. I usually keep it tidier than this, you know. I wanted to tell you that. With the holiday, it's been difficult to keep up with the cleaning the way I'd like, but normally it's quite tidy."

Esther smiled briefly, as though unable to hold the expression on her face.

"I hope you'll come more often," Louise said. "Mr. Harris would like it." She put a hand on the other woman's shoulder, removed it. "He sure loves you." The anger she'd felt earlier faded away. She felt sorry for Esther. "And he sure loved your mother."

Esther reached into her purse for her cigarettes. "Oh, he loves her, sure," she said. "Sure. He's very devoted, now that she's gone."

As WINTER BEGAN to give way, the grass on the lawn grew unruly and bright. Mr. Harris wet his trousers once, then again. Seeing him try to hide what he'd done threatened to break Louise's heart. She helped him undress and led him into the shower, averting her eyes as best she could. His body was pale white and spotted, ribs and thin muscles stark beneath skin. *If only Nan could see me*, she thought. He covered his face with his hands. She was very gentle about it, but still he flinched at the first touch of the washcloth.

"Well, don't stare at me," he said. "What are you looking at?"

She said nothing. His private place appeared heavy and soft, dampened by urine, achingly there. Seeing it, you felt the weight of yourself, the deep beauty and sadness of having a body.

She reached out and put the warm cloth in his hand.

"Wash your private place, Mr. Harris," she said. Then, because she had dared herself to, she said, "It's important you wash your penis as well."

It made her feel brave, saying that word, brave and loving toward him. She looked away as he lowered the cloth. There was holiness in the decay of the body, the dry, fragile shell of it, brittle, intact. She felt this and again thought of Nan. The lie had been given to something, at last. Steam rose, hot water fell on her dress. She wept with joy for the living and dead.

THE DAYS GREW warmer. Louise ventured outside. Increasingly, she took care with the lawn, ashamed of her prior neglect. It seemed a violation of their privacy that anybody driving by should be able to see such a clear, simple measure of the old man's decline. The work was arduous, but it was good to be out, and as she pushed the mower across the tall grass she felt the task was protecting them somehow, that its monotony helped to keep things in order.

She had gained weight during winter, cooking and eating proper meals every night. As a girl, she'd always been thin, even gaunt, and her appetite had been very poor. "Don't brush your hair," her nan had insisted. "Don't be a piggy," if she ate with relish. Thus had been Nan's disdain for the flesh: obscene, likewise, in sickness or health. Nan's life had been a project of slow self-erasure; Louise felt as though she were drawing herself. Before bathing each night she stood at the mirror, pale and naked, her arms growing soft at the shoulders. Her hands, scarred where she'd once chewed them raw, looked plump. Her wrists, too, where she'd cut them sometimes.

"Go out of the house when I've drunk the thing, girl," Nan had said on that final morning. Her eyes by that time had been sunken and grey, their whites the thick yellow of old mayonnaise. "Be seen. You're not to have touched anything."

Later, she'd come home to red and blue lights, emergency rung, the phone off the hook. When they'd asked her whether the body was Nan's, assent had seemed a betrayal of sorts.

Before the mirror now, she pinched the skin at her waist. "I can get a good deal fatter," she said, "before I give a thought to slimming again."

WHEN LOUISE BROUGHT Mr. Harris to his weekly appointments, she tried her best to accompany him. The seizures were causing further trouble with his speech. She answered questions, repeated advice, maintaining a weak charade of good health. The doctor must have seen things beginning to slip, but perhaps he also saw the affection between them, the way Louise held on to Mr. Harris's arm as she guided him through the surgery doors. He was gentle with her and with Mr. Harris: he never spoke of taking the old man from her charge.

"Why doesn't your daughter like to visit, Mr. Harris?" she asked him one evening after supper was cleared. "Why does she so seldom call?"

"I don't know." He didn't look at Louise. "I wasn't a very good father, I think."

"I don't believe that," she said.

"I'm afraid I must not have been." Distress seemed to tighten his throat.

"Were you very strict?"

"It was a different time, then," he said. "Everybody was strict with their children. We didn't know anything else. I never drank, if that's what you think."

Louise touched his large, papery hand. He still was not looking directly at her. "Of course not," she said. "Of course I don't think that." She wanted to say, "I love you, anyway."

IT BECAME TOO warm in the evenings for fires. Mr. Harris still watched his television programs, and Louise still read her books, but things were different without the glow from the hearth.

She opened windows, the front door as well. At times, she missed winter, but more often she was glad of the change. It felt good to have fresh air in the house. She took further to her work in the garden, not only mowing the lawn but spending hours some days pulling weeds, examining the grass from many angles until she was satisfied with its look. She bought a wheelchair at a secondhand shop and brought Mr. Harris outside with her. It was, she sometimes reflected, the happiest time in her life. They traveled short distances, up and down the block, and the thought of being seen with him in this way overwhelmed and delighted Louise. All winter she had been so fiercely protective of what they were building in the space of the house. Now with each step away from the door, she felt as if her heart would take wing.

"Mr. Harris," she said one evening in May, "would you like to sit outside on the porch?"

The days had grown to be languid and long; the sky was as pale as a scar.

He said nothing. She switched off the TV and helped him into his wheelchair, pushed him silently onto the porch. The concrete was swept and she sat down beside him, as she had all winter on the living room rug. On the street, cars went quietly past. People walked by with their dogs or with prams. She could hear faint music from a radio somewhere, like a whisper from the intimate past.

"It's dull out here," Mr. Harris complained. He appeared to be chewing at something. The seizures had taken a visible toll, so that he seemed always to be bracing for the next one now, as though flinching before a raised fist.

"It's a beautiful night, don't you think?" Louise said.

"It is," he said. "But I need my programs."

Louise smiled. Something was brimming inside her; it was not happiness, or fear, or love, or pity. It was not any of those things, exactly.

"Why do you need them, Mr. Harris?" she asked. "Why do you say you need them?"

He was looking down when he spoke. "I just really need them, Libby," he said.

At once overcome, she entered the house. In the hallway, she stood before the large picture, straightening the frame as Mr. Harris would do. She regarded it more closely than ever before: the faint dusty pattern of light on the bones and the way, even on the black and white film, it was clear that Libby's eyes had been green. A beautiful face. It resembled her saint's. For the first time, she recognized that. She remembered what Esther had told her at Christmas, but it did not change the way she thought about Libby or the marriage she had dreamed of these many months.

In the living room, she scanned the books for titles she knew. One by one, she began pulling them down, these dusty old things, this literature. As she lifted each book, she fanned through its pages, searching for a note, a dedication, anything in an unfamiliar hand. She knew that the light would be falling outside and that the old man would be restless. She worked quickly, the books laid in turn on the sofa.

It was inside the cover of *To the Lighthouse* that she finally found what she wanted. A careful and elegant script.

Elizabeth Harris, 1954.

Outside, at a distance, fog rolled off the sea, aching with light from the red setting sun. She turned on the single bulb next to the door to keep the porch lit when night fell in earnest and sat down again beside Mr. Harris. He looked at her, his eyes pale and opaque. She reached up and smoothed the cotton fabric of his shirtsleeve several times with the palm of her hand.

"Let me read to you, Wendell," she said, touching him a moment longer.

She began, then, to read aloud in the voice of another woman, as she had long imagined it. She felt as though she were taking part in a grand and exquisite drama. Mr. Harris remained silent, but she could tell he was listening. He had surely called her Libby as a simple slip of the tongue, or perhaps in a momentary confusion, but that was no matter. She read on. Her own attention faded in and back out, and it was difficult for her to follow the story, but that hardly mattered either. She was certain that this would be their way throughout the summer. If there came even the briefest of moments when the old man might believe he was beside his wife again, that would say more for the world than she'd ever have dreamed. And when they finished this book, she would find another and another and would read them slowly and quietly, until the last sun went down for them, after which it could never be said that she had failed to meet a good man, and to wed him, and to love him.

The Patroness

)( )( )(

Atelegram arrived as we were sitting to lunch, and Mrs. Hargreaves excused herself to receive it. I never liked it when she was called from the room, her presence being the only thing that justified my own, and relying as I did upon that skill of hers—which seemed to me a miracle then—at managing the conversation in a room or at table as if directing a sort of farcical play. I was the youngest there, yet to turn twenty, and already in the months I'd been attending her salon Mrs. Hargreaves must have saved me from a dozen encounters, whisking me off as though in intimacy, saying, "You're a saint to have endured that man as long as you did. He's a monumental bore, always has been, which was forgivable when he painted tolerably well, but between us, that's been some decades since." The other guests, now, seemed hardly to notice her absence: claret glasses were filled, cold meats and salad brought round on a platter.

"And your studies, Mr. Elford," somebody said.

I looked up, uncertain at first who had spoken. The faces arrayed about the table were pale; they blinked with equal measures of polite inattention.

"Going well, are they?"

The man who spoke was sitting opposite me, wearing the long, sober face of a horse: large nose, ears filigreed with tufts of gray hair. His profession, I recalled vaguely, had to do with the theater. It was at this moment that Mrs. Hargreaves might ordinarily have intervened, reminding everyone about my studies in maths, my particular interest in the art of the Bauhaus (the latter of which she had more or less invented for me, having latched on to a few nervous comments I'd made). "What Mr. Such-and-such is referring to," she might have begun.

"Very well, thanks." I smiled in his direction, sipped water in avoidance of further response.

I had begun attending Mrs. Hargreaves's salon at the arrangement of a mathematics professor who had served in the army with her late husband. It occurred biweekly on the ground floor of her house in Glebe Place, a gathering of what seemed not-quite-first-rate artists: playwrights and sculptors who'd sold work between wars, collectors and critics whose tastes had fallen from fashion. Still, to me it was impressive, indeed, my first glimpse of urban sophistication, embodied most of all in Mrs. Hargreaves herself, with her long and still-elegant figure, her pearls white beside the gray coif of her hair. All of this, and her magnificent house: these seemed to me as from a dream of the city, country lad—just in from Glass—that I was. I had found myself at university there, the closed doors of more ancient institutions having provided my young life's first indication that the world would not be offered so freely as I had sometimes allowed myself to believe. I had been a loner during the first term, feeling out of place and being given to worry: about my sister, still living at home; and about my father, who worked at the evaporated milk plant in Croft and who'd suffered some years with an affliction of the heart.

"She'll take to you and be a boon, I am sure," Professor Hastings had said of Dolly Hargreaves. "You're a mathematician by training but an artist at heart. Anybody would see that, my boy."

He smiled, though I could not help but perceive a small condemnation of my progress with partial differentiation. Nevertheless, it seemed a kindness that he had placed me in Mrs. Hargreaves's care, a kindness also that she should have accepted (a melancholy one in her case, perhaps, because the Captain and she had had no children of their own).

"Well you'll not guess whom I've heard from," she said, stepping back into the room. Her voice was like a songbird's, her face impish and flushed. "Why, it's Marina Valenska. Listen to this: 'Dolly, darling. In Cannes. Host has had temerity to drop dead at breakfast. Will come to visit you in England instead. Arrival by taxi in three days' time.'"

The other guests laughed, as I did, uneasily, wondering if a death had really occurred.

Mrs. Hargreaves took her place at the table.

I was seated beside a Madame Liselle DuPont, who had danced for a time in the Royal Ballet. She ate little, smoked from a cigarette holder. About her lips and her eyes were the finest sort of wrinkles, to which she'd applied a surplus of makeup. Her dress was a silk shift that hung loosely from her, the bones of her neck and her shoulders protruding.

"Twice divorced and once widowed, this Valenska," she said.

I nodded, my mouth full of food.

"You'll have known her from films. Or perhaps you are too young."

I can see now, recalling those days, that in addition to her generosity toward me, Mrs. Hargreaves used my presence for a kind of sport, for she liked particularly to seat me beside an aging beauty and to watch as I looked unthinkingly past her, performing the sort of casual, unwitting cruelty that the young sometimes do upon the old.

Ten days passed, and again my telephone rang. It was another summons to lunch.

"You'll be seated next to Marina, of course," Mrs. Hargreaves declared, and would hear nothing of my attempts to demur. "I think you will find her quite a fascinating woman. She was a lover to Stravinsky, Picasso, Valentino. You can talk about Bauhaus. She'll have known them all: Klee and Kandinsky. A great beauty in her day. She met Proust in Paris and loved him at first sight, though he was half dead and gay as a daisy, of course."

In my rooms, I read maths by the dim light of winter. I went to lectures, forgetting my umbrella, and came home with sodden clothes, stripping bare to be dried by the electrical fire. The scent of damp wool, the ache of fingers and toes as they warmed, aroused a homesickness in me, a want for Glass that my studies were powerless to distract. At home, on the hill looking over the sea, a wood fire, crackling, would throw fragile light; there, rain would be falling as well, like a whisper against the ancient thatch of the roof. On the boardwalk, neon lights of the penny arcade or the jazz club would be reflected in puddles. In the village, people would hurry about: Chris Blake, at work in his father's greengrocer, would lift crates or test fruit with unhurried ease, back straight as it had been on the pitches of our youth, a beauty which had agitated something in me; Pearl Bideford, beautiful also, in silk scarves and trench coat, would smoke beneath awnings. My only refuge from the weight of that longing was in dreams of this new, dazzling world I had glimpsed, its Turkish cigarettes and crystal decanters. And so all through that cold, dismal week, even shivering over dinners of baked beans and toast, my heart lifted at the thought of Marina Valenska: pitched forward at the edge of a symphony box, breast heaving, eyes brimming as she glimpsed her beloved, his pale hands and neck, that genius composer.

The day arrived, and I knocked just after noon on the great, shining black door in Glebe Place. It was answered by the same man who served at the table, Barnaby, who in the manifestations of his lifetime of work, and in the careful way his hair was combed to cover his baldness, reminded me of my father. He took my coat, my scarf, and my umbrella, the latter of which had been damaged in the wind.

"Ah, you're here."

Mrs. Hargreaves swept into the foyer.

"Good of you to come, braving the weather."

"Shocking," I said.

"Oh, but it is good. We'll be without Mr. Parsons," she said, referring, I realized, to the horse-faced man, "who, I'm afraid, cannot risk the damp air. And Madame DuPont, whom you will remember, has gone to Paris to visit relations. All the better because she'd not have forgiven me for denying her your company, and I so want you to speak with Marina."

I followed her down a corridor to the library, where we gathered every other week before lunch. The room was lit by only small, shaded lamps; oak shelving ran from ceiling to floor with a collection of gilt-embossed cloth and leather editions. A few guests sat, languid, on armchairs and ottomans, smoking and leafing through the pages in books. A poet, thirtyish, in a worn woolen suit, who Dolly had told me owed money to gamblers, stood alone by the window and polished his glasses. And there, at the center, as if of a vortex, splayed across an overstuffed, rococo settee, sat Marina Valenska, silent, ignored. Immediately, I recognized her, though she wasn't at all as I had imagined: grown old and run to billowing fat, draped in black chiffon and glistering jewels. I'd have laughed had I not been so strangely unsettled. She was posed for all the world as the star she had been: posture of sybaritic repose; cocktail glass, empty, held to her lips; expression of exaggerated, regal indifference.

She lifted her eyes when we entered the room.

"Marina, darling, here is the boy I told you about. A student, which no salon is rightly without."

Mrs. Valenska offered one hand to be pressed.

"Dolly's latest discovery," she said. "Dolly is forever making discoveries." Her pronunciation of the words was drawn out and British, marked with only the faintest Eastern European lilt, consonants softened as though by habituation to French.

I sat down on the extreme end of the sofa, nearest to where Mrs. Hargreaves still stood.

"Well, I don't know. There isn't anything to discover, I'm sure. We were introduced by Professor Hastings," I said.

"Well then you are a discovery of this professor, and Dolly has taken the credit. Very naughty of her to do that, but how can we blame her? You are a student she says. The mathematics, is it?"

I nodded. She went on.

"My father was friendly with Georg Cantor at one time," she said, and shifted her body a little, so that she sat more upright and nearer to me. Barnaby passed with a tray of fresh drinks, and she replaced her empty glass with a full one. "He came to the house a number of times, for parties rather like this." She gestured broadly, spilling some liquid. "I was, of course, too young to understand who he was, but I remember he had a bald head and behaved very strangely. He'd become a lunatic by that time, you know."

"I've heard that that happened."

"It is often the way." She said this and then seemed to grow pensive. There was an olive in her glass, and she regarded its distortion through the medium of the gin. From another room, down the long corridor, came the first tentative notes of a waltz, tapped out as though by a shy amateur asked to play for a professional's pleasure.

"Mrs. Hargreaves tells me you have known a great many important and interesting people." I glanced over my shoulder, vainly expectant of being rescued again, but our host had made her way to the window, where she spoke to the poet, who looked away, still not wearing his glasses.

"I've been acquainted with thousands, married to three. It would be truthful to say I've *known* some number between, though it's beastly of Dolly to have said so to you." She laughed.

Naive as I was then, I gathered her meaning. I could feel myself blush. "I have interest in the arts myself," I said, grasping. "The Bauhaus, for instance. Perhaps Dolly's told you."

"Yes, and I said it showed good taste, my dear. For my own part, of course, I have always adored Renoir, Seurat—people eating picnics, dancing and such. But for you, Mr. Klee is the better thing. The most mathematical of all the schools, would you not say?"

There had come into her eye a certain ghost of intelligence, an insouciant wit that must once have been attractive, in the days when it was more readily accessed.

"Yes, I suppose that's the trick of it," I said. "Appealing to the rational as well as to the artistic."

It might have been something I'd heard Dolly say; I don't really recall. I do believe I must have borrowed the thought, and yet saying it aloud seemed to make it my own. It was true I'd been moved by an oil on burlap hung in a modern gallery here. Why, then, should I not claim special interest? Why should I not hold an opinion? I had lifted, I realized, one foot from the floor, so that I was half recumbent, as Mrs. Valenska was. She reached listlessly as the drink tray passed on its return to the bar, removed the last remaining glass, and handed it to me. I drank, and she said, "Sense and sensibility, an Englishman might say. Always these go together, and always they are warring. It is true, isn't it, that the most difficult things in maths are often the simplest? One follows the line of most intricate thought, and finds that it leads back to the most basic truths. I think this is perhaps what drove poor Georg mad."

"And so Klee makes a harmony of them."

"Yes, yes," she said. "For you, he does. For me, it is perhaps Degas who does so. Or Renoir, or Manet. A simple portrait of a mistress, a whore. I have not so much of the analytical mind." She reached with two fingers to the bottom of her glass and lifted the olive into her mouth, pausing for an instant to savor the taste. "It is a wonder to me that your people seem only ever to paint landscapes and clouds, because it is they who need most of all to be made whole."

She rested the empty glass against the exposed skin of her chest, the other hand beside it, still wet with the gin. She was nearer still to me now; I saw the dye in her hair. The sharpness that had been for some minutes in her eye receded slowly, replaced by something vague but insistent.

"Ah," she said. "But you remind me of someone."

AT LUNCH, I was beside her as promised, she nearest to Mrs. Hargreaves, who presided again at the head of the long table. In form, everything was just as it had been two weeks before, and as it had been two weeks before that. The faces around the table had changed, as the subject of conversation surely would also, but the arrangement of bodies and the hierarchy it established, the way opinion was offered and deftly turned back, words spun out playfully and famous names tossed about, the repartee comprising a sort of battle to which my young mind could never quite measure but whose relation to the combatants' position within the salon I perceived—these things would be ever the same. Mrs. Hargreaves never meted out judgment or evinced her own opinion on these matters of hierarchy; to have done so would have fallen beneath her. She merely reflected in her delicate administration a consensus that the salon had already formed. Only I was allowed to exist apart from the fray, to offer nothing but my youthful and ragged appearance, and to sit, week after week, at the honored end of the table, indulged by Mrs. Hargreaves as a pet might have been, while professors and peers vied for approval.

Across the table, the poet sat furthest from her, with a literary critic and his wife, a Spanish tenor, and a journalist from a daily paper between them. To my left was an elderly man, a collector of antique figurines, whom Dolly always called Sir Ian, but with an ironic curl of the lip that made me wonder if his knighthood weren't somehow disputed; to his left was a dressmaker of some apparent repute; to my right, nearest Dolly, sat Marina Valenska.

Our glasses were filled by turns with white wine, and I gestured my acceptance when Barnaby paused, enquiring because I didn't usually drink. I thanked him. "Very good," he replied. There was a spot, I saw, near to his mouth that he'd missed with his razor and where a thin line of graying stubble remained. Again, briefly, I thought of my father; in Glass, he'd be smoking his pipe, perhaps recounting—while my sister half listened—a white flock of terns he'd glimpsed off the coast. (He fancied birds, the shock of their flight. Seeing them, tears might spring to his eyes.)

"A toast, then," Mrs. Hargreaves announced. "To Marina, who joins us today from abroad."

We lifted our glasses and drank.

"How many years, darling, since last you were here? We met, you understand," she said, addressing the room, "in Paris when I was there with Harold after the war. The Great War," she added, turning to me. "Marina was the most beautiful woman I'd ever seen."

There was a brief murmur of agreement with this, which Mrs. Hargreaves and Mrs. Valenska seemed equally to relish.

"Already, I had been to Hollywood then. I did not stay after falling out with Valentino. One is far too sensitive at that age, and I could not bear it. Of course it did not really matter: Talking pictures were anyway coming, and they would soon have found that my English was broken. How many years, Dolly? I think fifteen, perhaps."

"Well it's eleven this year since poor Harold is gone, so I should say that makes it a dozen at least."

"I recall, Mrs. Valenska," the dressmaker said, "seeing you in *The Golden Temple*. I was a girl, and I'd saved to go to the pictures. Of course I was taken with all of the costumes."

"Yes, I wore a dress with so many silks. They appeared golden and iridescent in the film, but in fact they were the most hideous green. You would not have approved of the design, I am sure. I took all my dresses home in those days—I liked them, and who was to stop me?—but I never took that one."

She smiled, revealing narrow, gray teeth, and afterwards took a long drink of her wine.

"I wonder what has become of them all."

We ate fish in a pale and rich sauce the likes of which I had not before seen. The wine was likewise rich and perfumed and seemed to me like the other finery in the house: something that I had no right to touch.

The critic and his wife had a child at Eton who would be reading greats at Oxford next year. "We hope he'll not try for highest honors," they said. "We feel it best he take up broader pursuits."

The journalist expressed his agreement. "Of course, I'll venture we took firsts ourselves. These ideas always occur to one later in life."

"Yes," said the critic, "but in our day the curriculum demanded wider reading. I fear that today it has narrowed, somehow."

Mrs. Hargreaves looked at me when this was said in the same ironic way she referred to Sir Ian, as if to say, "Are you not lucky to find yourself here, instead of surrounded by the sons of such people?"

"Ah, but we are quite left out of this talk of firsts and seconds, are we not, Señor?" Marina said to the tenor.

He was a man of about sixty years and a slightness of build that belied his profession. "It is true that we have not the same system," he said, not quite meeting her eye. "But I am in agreement that a formal education is insufficient alone. Do you not agree with this, Madam?"

"Do I not agree?" she said softly.

An uneasy silence presided. She might, for a moment, have been back on the stage. We watched her with a kind of hushed vigilance, as one would something dangerous, coiled.

"I, who was educated nowhere but in the drawing room of my father and on carriage rides through the streets of Vienna and Paris?"

She shifted, her voice increasing in force, red lips moistened with spittle and wine.

"Who have read the finest stanzas not inside of books but on pages torn from the manuscripts of the poets? Do I not agree? I, who claim no special knowledge of your field, Señor, but who have known the beauty of being serenaded under the moon by Caruso? Who felt the very voice of him tremble with longing? Who heard him later, after we made love in Venice, singing to himself in the bath? Do I shock you? Yes, I should say *I* agree. With such an education, how could *I* not agree?"

"A third it is, then?" Mrs. Hargreaves put in.

Audibly, our collective breath was released. We all laughed, except for Marina.

"I must apologize for the lack of discord. It would make for a livelier afternoon if there were some, but it is my principal weakness as host always to invite guests who agree with each other."

Discussion continued on similar topics, the critic and his wife holding dull court while the others offered occasional comment. Only Sir Ian and Mrs. Valenska showed no apparent interest at all. At length, she turned to me and said, too loudly, even as the critic's wife carried on, "And so, dear boy, you do not paint, yourself, but merely admire, as I do?"

"Oh, I've only done a bit of sketching," I said, whispering, trying not to draw further attention. "It's nothing to speak of. Maths is really the field of my study. I've no real expertise outside of it."

"It is good you should draw." She drank. Her glass had been refilled a number of times, and I saw that her sharpness, so briefly manifest earlier, had dulled further, and that the volume of her voice rose and fell as she spoke. "It is very good to be an admirer of art. This is all I have been since they stopped taking my picture. An admirer only. Always I surround myself with beautiful things. But to have attempted at least once to make something beautiful of your own: this is important. Dolly, the dear one, has not ever done so."

I looked at Mrs. Hargreaves, so near to us both, but saw no indication that she'd heard what was said.

"She has this salon, but she really knows nothing at all. It is an act. A play she puts on. That butler, he comes for these luncheons only. He is the man who trims the hedges outside. The cook, too. It is otherwise meat paste and rice. What other use has she got for a staff? But she feels she must give us this show. Oh, her eye is good enough; that much is true. It could not help but become so because of the Captain. He was very fine. People come to see her now because they need money or because they know they will encounter somebody they have interest in seeing. Others, like me, come because we were her husband's lovers, and we remember how he spoke of her in the darkness, how he pitied her and repented of all the bad things he had done, the cruel things he had said about her. We remember how he wished that she not be forsaken."

She placed a hand on the back of my own.

"But you do remind me of someone, dear thing."

I began to stammer something by way of response but faltered. A lull in the general discourse had left mine the only voice in the room.

"Marina," Mrs. Hargreaves said, "do include us in what you've been saying to Johnny." She smiled, and I could see, in the light of what Marina had said, that Mrs. Hargreaves, for all the elegance she had attained in her advanced age, all the knowledge and social skill she displayed, had been plain.

"The young boy and I were speaking about how strange it is that the British should not have had more painters of note," Marina said. She gestured in the direction of the Spaniard. "Of course, the same might also be said of their music." She paused a moment, waiting for the first inarticulate notes of objection to be raised, and when they were, politely, by the startled voice of the critic, she continued: "Ah yes, I know what you will all say. There are your darlings, like Constable and Elgar, whom you love because they tell you a fairy tale in which you are the princes. This is not the sort of art that I mean. Why, I ask, had Sisley to return himself to Paris in order to paint a proper picture of London? And why, for instance, has there been no great British painter of nudes, when the British need so desperately to be confronted with the nude form?"

I was aware painfully of her nearness and of the color that rose to my cheeks as everybody at the table turned their eyes on Marina. Her hand still rested on top of my own, and the certainty that they could all see this overwhelmed me with both thrill and revulsion. She drank again from her glass and reclined with satisfaction as far as the Edwardian stiffness of her dining chair would allow.

The critic's wife stabbed at her fish with displeasure. The dressmaker laughed mildly, said, "I should hope we never become *too* comfortable with such things, or I shall find myself out of a profession."

Mrs. Hargreaves clapped her hands and said, girlishly, "Ah, some disagreement, at last!"

"So you will approve, then," the journalist said, "of the young Freud, who seems to paint almost nothing but nudes."

"I approve of all Freuds, Monsieur. And yes, I thank God for the painter. But do not forget: He is born on the continent and so, I say, belongs to the continent forever."

"And Eliot, then?" the poet said, in a tentative voice. His fish, I noticed, had scarcely been touched.

"An American, of course. But I say nothing of your authors, who have always written well. I once played the part of Ophelia, you know."

Sir Ian, beside me, ate without taking notice. His hands were possessed by a delicate tremor and made noise when he applied fork and knife to his plate. Mrs. Hargreaves sat upright with a luminous smile, the strain of which was visible to me only later, in memory. I disengaged, gingerly, from Mrs. Valenska's grasp and lifted the glass of wine to my lips. I saw then, before I felt, that pale hand of hers removed from the table and placed gently upon my inner thigh; had I not, I might have choked at the sudden weight of it there. The critic was making a good show of keeping up conversation, expressing the rather pompous opinion that what Freud's work owed to his ancestral home was not nudity but its expressionistic aesthetic.

I excused myself from the table. The lavatory was at the far end of the hall onto which the dining room opened through a broad sort of archway; I moved quickly in its direction, conscious of the sound my shoes produced on the floor. I knew well my way about the downstairs and so was momentarily confused to find myself intercepted by Mr. Barnaby under pretense of his showing me to the washroom.

"See she doesn't have too much, won't you, sir?" he said, almost under his breath, when we were safely alone in the narrowness of the corridor. The walls were everywhere adorned with wainscoting and moldings; from the ceiling, at intervals, hung glass chandeliers. I must have looked perplexed by his question, because he added, "The Madam. The Russian lady, I mean. She's a good bit into the *vin blanc* already, and that's atop of what was served before luncheon."

"But I can't do a thing about that," I said. "You must see that I can't."

"Well if you don't mind, sir, she's taken with you, I'd say. That'd be a start. I'm obliged to serve her as she likes, aren't I? Only I don't like to see a lady suffering so."

His face, I could see now, was weathered and tan.

"And Mrs. Hargreaves? Surely she will say something."

"I'm rather afraid she'd welcome the show."

In the lavatory, I let cold water run over my hands. I was unaccustomed to even the small amount of drink I had had, and my reflection in the mirror over the sink seemed familiar and yet somehow not quite my own. The voices in the dining room were faint, indistinct, obliterated entirely when water rushed from the tap. I should have liked to stay there in the lavatory for some time, in its cool tranquility. I should have liked to stay until all the guests had gone home, until the lunch had been cleared and Mrs. Hargreaves retired, but soon there came, first vaguely and then with insistence, a tap on the door from outside in the hall. I wondered if it might be Barnaby, lurking, and inwardly I cursed him for slinking about, for having asked this thing so unfairly of me. I was a guest, and he had given me work, entitled because he knew I was a working-class boy. Because he could see that I didn't belong. It was just the same as when, one year before, I had cursed my father for coming with me to Cambridge when I was to have an interview there: it had not been that I was embarrassed by him, or that I felt him unworthy of anything, but rather that his presence had spoiled an illusion.

I dried my hands and opened the door. Before me stood Marina Valenska, her face pale and vacant as half-leavened dough. I had opened the door with some force, and she startled, a hand demonstrably brought to her breast.

"Ah, I've found you. But do not be angry," she said. One eye seemed to wander while the other was fixed.

"Not at all, only perhaps—"

She put the hand that had been on her breast to my lips, a clumsy gesture as suggestive of violence as seduction.

"But you remind me of him. It is a hard thing for an old woman to be reminded. Perhaps she can be forgiven it. He was my dearest lover, you know. The only one I would gladly have laid down my life for."

"Stravinsky?"

"A brute."

"I don't understand. Captain Hargreaves?"

"No." She made an impatient wave of the hand. "No, the boy. Boleslaw. My little William. I knew him in Paris. A Polish boy; a student, like you. I was thirty, and he was only seventeen. He was so wretched. He had only one suit of clothes, the poor thing. I bought him leather shoes and a wristwatch, but he was too shy to wear them. I made him drink coffee at Les Deux Magots. I heard many years later that he'd become a soldier. Ah! How frightened he must have been. He used to lie between my legs like a puppy, you know."

She said this wistfully and in a moment grew somber.

"I was beautiful then. They will have told you."

"And what happened to him?"

"How can I know?"

"How did the love affair end?"

"As they all do, my boy. How stupid you are. How lovely, and stupid, and exquisite, and cruel."

She had begun to weep, and the billows of black fabric draped over her person lifted and fell again irregularly so that she looked like something wounded but living, glimpsed at some distance amid a desolation. When she kissed me, I allowed it to happen, allowed the full drunken weight of her to fall in upon me. It was not pity that compelled me, or not that alone. She smelled of perfume and gin; she was clammy to touch. She kissed me desperately, urgently, right there in the doorway to Mrs. Hargreaves's lavatory, and all the time she whispered, "Ah, my dear, my lovely."

It was the first time I'd been embraced by a woman since the day, ten years before, when my mother had died.

When, at last, she drew away and my faculties reestablished themselves, I became aware of the black and white figure of

Barnaby looming just beyond the rise of her shoulder. Behind him, where the dining room gave onto the corridor, stood the whole of Mrs. Hargreaves's salon, assembled: the dressmaker stifled a laugh; the critic and his wife did their best to feign scandal; the writer cast about his professional eye, taking in every sordid detail; the tenor yawned as though he'd seen such things before; the poet merely adjusted his glasses; Sir Ian puzzled over the face of his watch, embarrassed or maybe indifferent; and over them all presided our host, Mrs. Hargreaves, as ever composed. She clasped her hands at her waist and tilted her head in a school-matronly posture of mock disapproval.

"Why, Marina, you really are *too* incorrigible. I shouldn't think a love affair had commenced over a bit of talk about painting and a few bites of haddock. Did I not say you were free to seduce whomever you liked, with the sole *exception* of Mr. Elford, who is far too young and too good for such things? You've frightened him half to death, my dear woman. He looks like a hare that's heard a step in the grass."

The doorway remained open behind me, and with one step I could have slipped into the darkness. To be invisible, just for one blessed moment, would have been a monumental relief, but it would also have been too cruel to Marina, who had turned, miserably, to face Mrs. Hargreaves. It seemed that a great deal of time passed in silence, broken only by Sir Ian, who snorted into a handkerchief. At last, Marina, standing unsteadily now, moved with dignity to smooth the chiffon of her dress. It was easy, watching her then, to believe that here was a woman who had had many lovers but only one fleeting love in her life.

"I was reminded," she said, as though to no one at all. "There is no crime in being reminded."

Another interval passed, and she lifted her head. She looked to Barnaby, who had drawn himself nearer.

"Mr.—" she said.

"Barnaby, Madam."

"Would you be kind enough to take me to where I might lie down?"

"Certainly, Madam," Barnaby said, and he took her by the soft, hanging flesh of an arm. They walked gingerly, hunched over a little, like a couple together in the dusk of their life.

Marina leaned closer, whispering something.

Barnaby nodded, whispering back.

OUTSIDE, DARKNESS HAD fallen and I walked in the rain, only vaguely protected by my damaged umbrella. The orbs of warm light from the lamps appeared large, distorted, as the green olive had in her gin. At home, I paused before reaching my rooms to scrounge a cigarette from a neighbor. "Been out in this?" he said. "See you don't catch your death." I leaned against the frame of his door as if it were the only thing holding me up.

"Thank you," I said. The words caught in my throat. I left him without saying anything else.

I lit the cigarette at the electrical stove. I'd left the wireless on, the volume low enough to have escaped my notice before; it carried on now with an orchestral piece. My thoughts wandered but never strayed very far. The cool touch of Marina's lips and of her body remained, a presence, it seemed, as real as any other. I'd been confronted, as she said every Englishman must, with the physical form, not nude but shrouded in the most delicate fabrics. This, she'd suggested, had the power to make one whole. So why, then, did I feel so totally shattered?

ANOTHER WEEK PASSED; the rain dissipated a little. Exams were approaching, and I busied myself with my studies. I did not hear from Marina at all, though there were many things I would have liked to ask her: about solitude, about the things she regretted, about Proust on a rainy sidewalk in Paris.

I spoke with my sister for a time on the phone. Chris Blake had taken her out. She was shy, but I heard the note of thrill in her voice. Cream teas along the boardwalk, a film; he'd loaned her his coat when it rained. "It's what's meant," my father said on the subject. "I'll manage, sure enough. Don't fret about that."

I did not know whether or not I ought to expect another summons to Mrs. Hargreaves's salon, nor whether I wished to receive one. But it came, just as ever it had, in the middle of the following week.

"I didn't know if you'd want me back," I said.

"Nonsense. You've become a fixture of our little luncheons. Madame Dupont will be back, as will Naismith, the poet."

"With the gambling debts," I said rather vaguely. I was standing by the window, looking onto the street. It was midday and people bustled about.

"I've paid those, I'm afraid," Dolly said. "Oh, I oughtn't have. He'll only accrue more, but he's still young and occasionally turns out a good verse. I couldn't bear to see him beaten about the knees or thrown into the streets. It's too awful for that sort of thing to happen to a poet."

"And Mrs. Valenska," I said. "Will she be at the luncheon?"

"Ah, my dear, no. You needn't worry. How polite you are, waiting so long to ask. Marina left me at the end of last week. I believe she was off to Italy next."

I sat down in the small wooden chair from my desk, which I placed sometimes just next to the window. I experienced, when she said this, a strange sense of loss.

"I rather thought she'd still be there," I said.

"Oh, no. She's not one to linger. Not after she's got what she came for."

"What she came for?"

"Why, money, of course. The same as the poet. Same as all of them, darling. They come for money; isn't that what she told you? Or did she say pity? Well I suppose that's true, too; a widow must always accept people's pity. We're all parasites of one kind or another. What Marina needed, though, was money. She hasn't a bean of her own. The dead husband, it turns out, was simply buried in debt, and the divorces, well, you can imagine: she was hardly in a position to ask anything of *them*. She got what she wanted, but I dare say she paid a fair price. I rather think you destroyed her, my dear."

On the street, a man was getting into a taxi. A woman was standing and watching him go.

"She said she had once been Captain Hargreaves's lover."

"Oh, that's true. Doubtless it is. Marina is proud, and lecherous—sometimes I wonder if she isn't a bit mad—but if she told you she was my husband's lover, you may rely upon its being the truth. Why, if I'd had any doubts, I wouldn't have given her a tuppence, I'm sure."

"I don't understand."

"No," Dolly said. "No, I should think not."

CERTAIN THINGS ABOUT those days would never become clear: the deepest mysteries of number theory and logic, what a butler might have whispered to a suffering guest.

But the passage of time can render some things comprehensible. I did, for instance, come to understand what Marina had meant when she said that all love affairs end the same way. Like her, I came to know the pain of being reminded, the liquid beauty of Degas's ballerinas, the ache that occurs in a scarred, aged heart at the tender depiction of an immodest nude. Such things do, as she promised they would, make us whole, but for one instant only, for we are all broken beings and far past repair.

My sister married Christopher Blake and never seemed to outgrow her shyness about him. I suppose I never really outgrew mine, either. My father carried on for many years by himself, his heart proving not so weak after all. When he died, he did so alone, as the papers reported Marina had, too. I read the stories on the train back to Glass, where in two days' time we would bury my father (and where I would find myself estranged by long absence, unrecognized in that place I had loved). Ruined actress, they said. Twice divorced and once widowed. A socialite fallen on difficult times. Nowhere did they mention a young refugee, a Polish boy, a gift of leather shoes or a watch. Nowhere either was mentioned the kiss she had shared with a student of maths or the impression of her lips that had lingered on his face to return sometimes for no reason at all as he lay, sleepless, through the years of his life. Unmentioned, lastly, was the salonnière who had shown her at once such generosity and malice, that woman whose eye had indeed been sufficient to recognize something fine when she saw it and who had had, thus, grudgingly to accept that the moment of joy, of wholeness, that her husband had once found in wanton embrace had been one worthy, at last, of her patronage.

Other People's Love Affairs

❌ ❌ ❌

For twenty years, Erma and Violet lived together in Glass, neither simply as friends nor precisely as lovers. If ever a question on the matter was raised, or if (more often) assumptions were made, they would share a glance, blushing, without a reply, not having a name for what they were to each other. Corpulence distinguished them both, indeed was something that had drawn them together, though Violet carried hers with superior ease. They shared a room in a half-timber cottage, two twin beds with a table between. They liked books, jigsaw puzzles and games, videos saved of *Not Only . . . But Also*. Each night, turning out the lamp before bed, Erma would say, not shyly,

"I love you, Violet," and then listen for a time to her friend's moving lips as she proceeded through a whispered nightly devotion. Had she ever managed the words, what Erma might have said of their union was that neither of them had ever truly been cared for, except in these last years by the other. There was nothing in them really worthy of love, the world had for so long seemed to say; it had stopped saying that on the day when they met. Now, listening in the darkness, Erma was often moved, overcome, knowing it was she who rated highest among Violet's prayers.

Sex had never come into things, at least not in a conventional sense. It wouldn't have, in Erma's case, being something she had long ago ceased to consider. (Aged eleven, she'd pined briefly after Phineas Cork, the only boy in school who hadn't thought it was funny when she sat in the butter cruelly spread on her chair; later, she'd watched others court and be married, feeling only the mildest envy.) That she had wound up with another woman for a companion seemed perfectly natural and predictable to her, but she never considered it the like of other people's love affairs.

Mostly, they displayed only passing affection, notwithstanding Erma's avowals. Only once had they breached that convention in earnest, when news had come that Violet's mother was dead.

A telegram had arrived at the house: an odd, archaic thing, even then. In the kitchen, Violet slowly sat down. She handed the paper to Erma.

It was strange: they'd lived together for years, and she hadn't known Violet's mother was living.

That night, for the first time, they shared a bed.

"My poor mum." Violet trembled with grief. She lay on her side with her face to the wall.

"Oh, dear one," Erma said. "You dear thing." The curtains, gossamer, blue, did not move. With her own body, she traced the curve of her friend's.

No prayers were said in their house on that night. Together, they breathed; one's hand clasped the other's. The sea could be heard where it battered the cliffs.

ABOUT THE SMALL coastal village of Glass they were known, traveling together in their pale yellow Beetle. Violet drove; people waved as they passed; smiling back, she tooted the horn. The car had been hers originally, as the house they lived in had been as well, possessed jointly since shortly after they met at the library, where Violet was in charge of collections and where Erma had a habit of running up fines. You got to know people in that line of work, as you did in Erma's, too, selling paper and cards. They were friendly with local shopkeepers and clubs: with Herville, the butcher; with the Women's Institute ladies; with Trilby, the florist, until she shut down.

Meals were their own form of intimacy, a shared time calling them back to the body. Together, they cooked elaborate dishes: meat pies and hearty soups every winter; grilled fish, potato salads in summer. They had large appetites and did not pretend otherwise, as Erma felt they both must have done in the past. In the kitchen, as elsewhere, Violet directed, and though Erma was the more experienced cook, she didn't mind being told what to do or even a harsh word now and then. Sometimes when it grew hot in the kitchen Violet would strip right down to her bra. "Don't mind, do you, love?" she'd casually say, and then ask for a spoon or a bowl that she needed. "Don't find it's too much distraction?" She might sing a song, do a shimmy. "Your Feet's Too Big" or "Roll Out the Barrel." When Erma laughed, she covered her mouth; when Violet did, she threw back her head and her whole body tumbled in a beautiful manner, like water suspended for an instant in space.

AND THEN, ON the cusp of their twenty-first year, Violet's heart failed her as she'd been warned it would do. Through the years, Erma had tried sometimes to institute diets, not wanting one herself, nor to spoil their pleasure, but frightened of being left alone in the end. Being younger by several years, she'd been burdened by the possibility of that.

They'd gone for lunch to a café they liked by the sea. In the sun, overlooking the long, rugged coast, the vendors and Ferris wheel on the strand, they had eaten crab legs with buttered rolls and white wine while gulls circled and landed nearby.

"I'd like anything you ate with a hammer," Violet said. She laughed and pounded the table. "All I need is a robe and a wig."

Afterward, they walked a trail near the shore, and it was there, in the dappled shade of an oak, that Violet collapsed, slowly, first to one knee and then further, with a plaintive glance over her shoulder, until she was laid out, quietly prone.

Erma rushed to her, nearly crippled with panic. The space around them was terribly still. She removed the cellular phone from her pocket, shaking as she pulled it open and dialed. Later, she would not recall what was said or how long she'd waited that way on the line. She would remember only how she held Violet's hand, which was moist and scarcely able to grasp.

"You dear thing," she said. "Oh, heavens. Oh, lord."

Soon, people came and shouted for help. A small crowd gathered; she wished they would go. One man placed his hands between Violet's ribs and pressed while his wife held Erma away. From their place on the ground they could see nothing of the ocean and only the barest patch of the sky. Paramedics arrived with a board and a gurney; they placed a mask over Violet's face. At some point, the top of her blouse was pulled open, and Erma wailed, wanting to cover her friend, shy for her in this state of undress, which only she herself had been allowed before to see.

When, passing through the Mercy Hospital doors, she was informed that Violet had died, Erma's first thought was that the end of her own life might as well come, and that, when it finally did, she would never—not even once—have been kissed.

VIOLET HAD MADE a formal accounting, though she didn't own much beyond the house they had shared. The will was in a safe deposit box in the city, which had to be opened by a long-estranged cousin, a woman who did not resemble Violet at all and who grumbled about the task, perhaps guessing that she would be unmentioned in the document. Catharine her name was. She came to the house, meeting Erma with a curious eye.

"I suppose I knew her quite well as a kid," she said as they drove to the bank.

They had turned up Douglass, heading out of the village. A thick fog was rolling in off the sea. Outside the butcher's shop, Herville was sweeping; Erma wondered if he had been told.

"Haven't seen her for ages, though, really. I understand she let things go in the end."

Erma didn't say anything. She hadn't any idea what Catharine could mean, unless she was referring to weight. The thought that there might have been talk about Violet, even gossip, among the unknown figures of her past was upsetting. Erma had not concealed a world of family, old friends; she'd had none of those things when they met. That had been at a very low time, when she'd moved to Glass with what money was left from her parents, two people who had tried to be kind but who'd never managed to disguise their disappointment with life. They had died some two weeks apart, not because the one remaining (her father) could not bear to go on without the other but because, in widowerhood, he had been relieved of a burden and had no obligations left to the living. She felt her parents would have left their house and their money to somebody else if they could have but had settled for her as they'd settled for other things, too: because it had been their duty to do so.

At the bank, Catharine entered the vault while Erma was left to wait in the lobby. The floors were polished to a high, mirrored gloss; she squinted, avoiding the glare from the lights. She ate a mint from her purse, blew her nose. She would have liked very much to be named next of kin. It had seemed only natural to her that she should be, but it turned out there were rules about that.

In the days since it happened she had not managed sleep. It was terrible to be in the bedroom, the empty twin bed beside her, sloppily made, as she'd so often reproached Violet for doing. In the darkness there was only her own breathing, sometimes the sea, and she longed for the sound of her friend's muted prayers. She could not even re-create them in her mind, unable somehow to recall ever having made out a word of invocation. What she did recall was the quietness of it and the stillness she had felt while she listened: Violet, the buoyant and riotous one, transformed in the final moments of day.

THE WILL, IT turned out, contained a small curiosity.

Everything had been left to Erma, without specification, excepting one item she'd all but forgotten. This was a damaged rolltop desk, a large and cumbersome walnut antique, that had been covered over with a dust cloth in the garage for as long as Erma had lived in the house. It was to be given to a man named John Killian, owner of the Green Man in Hart Street. Erma knew at once who he was, having been sometimes for a drink at the pub: a tall fellow, balding and painfully thin; he was friendly, an easy and good-natured man, but hardly someone they'd ever remarked on.

He turned up at the funeral but drew no attention. He wore black, placed a small bouquet of narcissus on the card table that had been arranged for the purpose. She had settled on a casual service, not lengthy or strictly religious, recalling that Violet had been brought up Catholic, but never having known her to confess. (Her prayers, she reasoned, had been of a general sort.) Cremation had been Violet's wish, a release from the body for which she'd been known. Afterward, people milled about for a while. They took Erma's hand, expressed their condolence, but stopped short, it seemed, of treating her as a widow.

She wrote to him one week after the service: a brief note detailing the gift, no query as to what its meaning could be.

Days passed. Life was dreamlike and strange. Evenings, she felt odd attempting to cook; her hand gripped the knife where Violet's had, too. In the wash, some of her things were still there, the last time that would ever be so. In town, Mr. Herville sliced too much bacon; Ault reached, by habit, for a bottle of Port, forgetting that only Violet had drunk it. She didn't linger in those shops anymore. It had been Violet, she saw now, who'd established their friendships, Violet who'd been fun, flirtatious even, who'd pulled faces, winked, said clever things.

After dinner, she often went out to the garage and stood awhile in the dim, fusty light. She regarded the desk, still covered at first, then with the dust cloth thrown to the floor. The finish was scarred, the wood chipped away; there wasn't anything left in the drawers.

Returning to the house through the backdoor one night, she heard the phone in the living room ring.

"Erma."

She recognized Killian's voice: high-pitched and roughened by smoke in the bar.

"Thank you," he said. "For letting me know."

A foghorn sounded away in the harbor.

"Well, I only wanted to check. Ask you when the best time would be," he said.

"The best time?"

"To haul it away."

She was silent. He might have acted surprised. That would have been the kind thing to do. It was all so strange; beyond fathom, really. She said, "Oh, I'm sure I don't mind."

A puzzle, unfinished, lay spread on the table. Bruegel, a white and wintry scene. Violet had laughed as she scoured the pieces, hunting for bare buttocks, revelry, mischief.

"Come whenever you like," Erma said. "It won't make the least bit of difference to me."

AND SO HE arrived in a tweed suit, a tie, a rumpled walking hat held in his hand. In the doorway he stood, nervous, irresolute; with a briefcase and a stack of brochures he might have been a beleaguered salesman, a proselytizer. He had backed a small van against the door to the garage, the way she had instructed him to. It was borrowed, he said, from a friend in the hills, his own car not large enough for the job.

"You were the only other person named in the will," she said as she followed him down the front steps.

It was midday; the sun was high and benignant. She bent down slowly to lift the garage door.

"Strange, that, wouldn't you say? Of course, there were good times had in the pub, but I wonder why this desk of all things."

He looked down. "I admired it once."

He'd brought a dolly for lifting the desk, and she helped him tip the front end up off the ground. The old wood was heavy; she was obliged to press her whole weight against it, to strain further as she helped him guide it into the van along a short metal ramp he had borrowed as well.

"I should have brought somebody with me to help," he said.

She was breathing hard with exertion. They both were. Wisps of hair clung to her face.

"It was wrong of me, making you do it," he said. He slapped a fly at the back of his neck. In the wake of their effort, his shyness had grown.

"Oh, no, no," was all Erma managed. She did not want him knowing how she minded it all: his coming, his driving away with the desk, or the damage wrought by her realization—firm and inescapable now—that Violet had been in love with him first.

SUMMER LINGERED AND then finally broke; the trees throughout Glass surrendered their leaves. Through all the autumn months, she was visited by the humiliating thought that the night spent sharing one bed with Violet had for her friend been eclipsed by the love of a man. That she knew this man, had spoken to him in Violet's presence, made it all the worse. She wondered if they had laughed about her in secret, for it was possible the affair had carried on to the end; she thought of Killian on the front step, hat in hand: Had he looked like a man whose lover had died?

The first time she parked outside the Green Man was on a gray evening in early November. The cobbles of Hart Street were slick, iridescent; lamplight caught wide swaths of delicate rain. That week, she'd seen a whale breach off the coast—a wild, heart-rending, beautiful thing, rare because it was late in the season—but no one had been there to witness it with her. On the radio, now, a program was on about a man serving a life term in prison whose paintings sold for fabulous sums. A critic said they could move you to tears. She lifted her fingers to warm at the fan.

Idling, she regarded the pub: the Dutch door, the yellow fruit machine light. She thought of Violet drinking there, years ago, before they had met one another: laughing, leaning over the bar to whisper something in Killian's ear.

For her there had been the kind boy at school, as well as film actors: Paul Newman and such. But those sorts of things were undeniably different. She had never cooked dinner with anyone else, never fallen asleep beside anyone else. It would not even have been worse to find that Violet had loved another woman in her life, because at least then she would know it hadn't repulsed her to be touched by one.

A couple came walking out of the pub and turned up Hart Street in Erma's direction. They didn't have an umbrella. The man wore an overcoat, holding it open; the woman stood near while he wrapped it around her. Erma turned the radio down. In silence, she watched them move, hunched in the rain. It was nothing for them, plainly, to stand close in this way, nothing to kiss, as they paused once to do. She could hear, as they passed, the sound of their steps and of their voices: whispering, laughter. She could see the woman's small wrists, her pale calves, and her face lifted to the man's—a bare offering—and all of it seemed ostentatiously to proclaim, "We are lovers! We are lovers!"

She slouched down in the driver's seat (a seat that still did not feel rightfully hers) and listened until their footsteps had gone. She did not look again at the pub before pulling onto the wet, cobbled road, but she glanced up, just once more, as she passed it, heading in the direction of home.

THERE WOULD BE other visits to the tavern that winter, glimpses stolen through windows and doors of John Killian: serving drinks, changing a cask. If she stayed until close she could see him lock up, wave goodnight to any bar staff who might have been on. He would pause then and turn up his collar, use it to shield a cigarette from the wind. Sometimes, when he had got in his car, she would turn the key softly to ignite her own engine and follow the glow of his lights at a distance.

Why she watched, what it was she was hoping to see, she did not know. He never strayed from routine: never drove off in the company of a woman, never turned left where he should have turned right. Often she phoned the pub from inside the car, but when he answered she found herself with nothing to say.

December. Streetlamps were furnished with garlands, the Green Man with strings of bright colored lights. She and Violet had never really made much of Christmas, but they'd enjoyed their simple routine: a bottle of champagne, Richter's good panettone, and, if Violet was feeling nostalgic, a walk past the church to listen at mass. What pained Erma now, as the holiday neared, was not simply the end of these things; it was the belief that, in her own absence, Violet would have managed to carry them on. For it was clear now that to Violet they had merely been roommates, bound first of all by convenience and thrift. How foolish Erma had been. That most everything had been left to her was hardly any consolation at all; she'd got that because it was only fair that she should, the same as when her parents had died. The greater gift, it seemed to her now, had been Killian's, precisely because it was worthless, because it was no more than a symbol. In this short, meager life, it is a thousand times rarer to be given what isn't owed.

WHEN SHE TELEPHONED Catharine it was midday, though Erma had not yet been out of the house. Outside, the landscape was fogged in and dreary. The sea and the sky were a similar gray. There was a pot of leftover soup on the stove, bread to warm in the oven for lunch. It took a moment to explain who she was; they'd not spoken since the will was retrieved.

"I thought I'd tell you how I was getting on," Erma said. "And how the town remembers her. They still wave at the car when I pass. They forget, you see. Friends everywhere she went, Violet."

"Yes."

"Was she always that way? When you knew her, I mean?"

"I suppose she was," Catharine said. "She was a prettier girl than you'd think."

"So she wasn't always plain?" Erma said. She pictured Violet, laughing and near. She'd been the taller between them, the fairer. "I was, always."

Catharine made no reply.

"And she had a good sense of humor?"

"Yes, of course," Catharine said. "But you know that, Erma. You knew her a longer time than I ever did."

Erma smiled hearing that and let the silence stretch a moment over the line. She was in the sitting room of their house, curtains drawn to the fog, the fire unlit. It had been she who'd split wood for them winters, having learned the proper way from her father, a job that more often a man would have done.

"Erma," Catharine said. "Why have you called?"

"She must have been popular," Erma went on. "With boys, I mean."

"That was part of the trouble."

There had been girls she'd admired, too, Erma thought now. From the far past there emerged an image of one, books clutched tight to a pretty white cardigan, skirt ballooning away from her waist. The sort of girl who might smile at you from a distance or offer to show you how makeup was worn, who might suggest asking a boy to spring ball, never thinking those things could be hurtful to say.

"She left home after school?"

"She never finished," Catharine said. "I'm surprised you didn't know that." There was, for the first time, some cruelty in her voice. "Once she left, she never came back."

Erma was reminded of all the many occasions she'd been surprised by some item from Violet's past, as though assuming she'd not have had one at all, or that, as a matter of course, it would have matched exactly her own. That belief had been another part of the foolishness, for what in life had ever suggested that she might so possess her beloved? She should have recognized Violet, having seen her before: no different from the girl in the skirt, the kind boy; she'd been generous, loving after a fashion, but finally remote, beyond grasp.

"I held her all night when her mother died," Erma said. She had never told anybody before. "I held her and kissed her neck while she wept."

Catharine sighed. She was silent a moment, and then she said, in a voice no longer cruel but exhausted, "I nursed Violet's mother through the whole of her suffering."

By the time they had each said good-bye and rung off, the fog had given way to a rain. It fell steadily, softly, without any purpose, a sound like handfuls of dry, scattered seed. Erma stood, relit the stove for her soup, feeling she might stay in after all.

IN THE NEXT days she didn't return to the pub. It was not that she wished to let go of Violet or surrender the memory of her to Killian. Only she felt that the point had been reached where there wasn't anything left to be learned. There was solace to be taken in one thing, at least: that the biggest changes of her life had already occurred.

And yet, as happens, despite her resolve, she did see John Killian again: a mere ten days later when, in the evening, she answered the door and was met with his figure. He was dressed in the same ill-fitting suit, the same tie, the overcoat she'd seen on so many nights. This time he was still wearing his hat, and it cast his face into deadening shadow.

"Now look here, Erma," he said.

She stepped back, aware of her own beating heart, her own ribs.

"What are you after, ringing the pub? Slinking about, following me? I don't like it. I've a mind to see the police."

Momentarily, she tried to muster some anger: he'd come to her home, unannounced. What she found, though, instead, was embarrassment, shame. Her shoulders fell; she lowered her head. It did not cross her mind to tell him a lie, as it never had, really, in all of her life. Seeing her face now, one might have wondered if its lack of beauty had forever been a consequence of inability to deceive.

"Come inside, Mr. Killian," she said. "Come inside, John."

In the sitting room, he seemed slowly to alter. She watched him with his hands in his pockets, blinking as he regarded it all: the unfinished puzzle, the jars of glass beads, the doilies and antimacassars on chairs.

"I'm having potato dumplings for supper."

He frowned, puzzled, seeming not to have heard.

"I haven't shared a meal these six months."

She took his coat and his hat, led him into the kitchen. At the far end of the corridor was the bedroom, but she didn't say that, knowing he knew.

On a pan, she arrayed the small yellow pies. She motioned for him to have a seat at the table, and when she'd put the dumplings in the oven, she joined him.

"How long has it been since last you were here?"

"Decades," he said. "Twenty years, Erma."

From the sadness in his voice, she believed him.

"The desk was in the bedroom, those days."

They were quiet. He put his hands on the table. One wrist was broader than the other one was, irregular in shape, as though from arthritis. It would have bothered him lifting the desk. She wondered how he'd managed once he'd gotten it home.

"I'm sorry I lurked at the pub."

"I thought you'd gone mad."

"I didn't mean trouble." She shifted her gaze, not allowing it to rest on his face. "How did you find me out?"

"The car, Erma." It almost seemed as if he would laugh. "Everybody recognizes that car."

She smiled and glanced at the clock. "Not exactly double oh seven, I guess."

At length, she rose to take the food from the oven, returning with two plates of dumplings, two forks. She offered a beer, and he accepted.

"It was hard when I found you were named in the will."

She sipped her own beer, wiped the foam from her lip.

"It was something she'd kept a secret from me, which I never liked thinking she did."

Killian nodded. Steam rose from his plate where he'd opened a dumpling with the side of his fork.

"She loved you, I suppose," Erma said.

His chewing slowed, and she recognized in him the feeling she'd come to know in these months: the almost overwhelming weight of the heart, the way food became like a stone in the mouth.

"I drove her home in the evening sometimes," he said. "She drank too much in those days. She was mistreated."

It no longer shocked Erma hearing that said, only saddened her. "She was prettier then?"

"Maybe she was, but it was never just that. You know what she was like. Sometimes, when I put her to bed she would say something sweet to me," he said. "But she was as likely to say something cold."

"It's terrible finding you were wrong about someone." She did not want to eat. She was thinking of Killian sitting alone at the desk beside Violet's bed. Listening, waiting for her breath to find a rhythm.

"I'm glad she never told you about me," he said. "It wasn't easy pouring drinks for the two of you, seeing you in the passenger's seat of that car. I'm glad Violet and I had one thing to ourselves. It's only fair, Erma, since you got all the rest."

"Oh, no, no," she said, as she had also on the day when he'd come for the desk.

She cleared their plates. He thanked her and stood, though it seemed he might like to stay a while longer.

As she showed him out, as they exchanged apologies and condolences, as they even embraced in the doorway, Erma knew that in John Killian's eyes it was she who'd had the better end of things, who'd won Violet's heart and what time there had been. He did not know, as all the other people of Glass did not either, that her endearments had gone for twenty years unanswered, that the desk in the bedroom had been replaced not by one large bed but by the addition of a second twin. When they'd waved at the car as it passed on the road, they had all thought or spoken aloud, "There is Violet with her Erma." And when Violet had sounded the horn they had taken it for a proclamation of love. They need never find now how mistaken they'd been; what they believed had in time become its own truth. This was the gift that Violet had given in death, having been unable to offer what was asked for in life. It was quite a lot. Nearly everything, really. For Killian, there was only the desk and the memory of things whispered in the darkness of a room: thanks offered vaguely as breath through the lips; prayers from the world between waking and dreams.

The Well Sister

ꕤ ꕤ ꕤ

Friday evening, slowed by an ache in his foot, Myron Idris climbs the narrow flight of steps to his room. He pauses a moment, reaching the top, long enough for the overhead bulb to shut off. Outside, the day has only just begun waning, but in the windowless stairwell it is too dark to see. He curses, setting his bags on the landing, waves an arm in hopes of restoring the light. For months he tried to dissuade Mrs. Usak from having the motion sensor installed. It has only been a nuisance, as he knew it would be; there was never anything wrong with the switch. But she was insistent—"For safety," she said—and finally he surrendered his case. He is liked downstairs, given a discount, because he isn't the sort of person who presses a point. If his chicken is dry or lettuce has gone off, he only mentions it once, and shyly at that. He is a model tenant, in many respects. Twice he has mended the faucet himself; he is always on time with the rent.

He fumbles to place his key in the lock, relieved when he feels it settle into its groove. A clatter of dishes can be heard from below. They'll be preparing for the first rush of dinner: oil brought up to heat in the fryer, the rims of glasses inspected for stains.

The room, when he enters, smells warmly of rot; it is time he took the rubbish down to the street. A lamp beside the sofa is lit, and he curses again at the thought of his bill.

On the counter, he arrays the items he's bought: tuna fish, baked beans, custard, and peas. Bananas he hangs on a hook beneath the dish cabinet; a whiskey bottle goes beside the dwindling one. The kitchenette is in need of a cleaning. The whole room looks suddenly shabby to him. That happens when you are gone all day from the house: you come back and see your own life as if from afar. It would not do to bring the woman from the thirty-six here, any more than it would to have brought the one from the bookshop.

And so he sets about cleaning the space, the rubbish bag knotted and placed by the door, surfaces dusted and wiped with a rag. He moves slowly, having nowhere to be, taking care because he is the sort of person who does.

With a smile, he remembers saying, "Rain again," displaying the screen of his cellular phone. That memory has been with him all day, through his half shift at the bookshop and at the market as well. She was riding the bus as he'd known she would be: the thirty-six, going north to the city center. Mornings, she works in a publishing house, a local one, small books of poetry, mostly. He knows because he followed her there, unable to believe his good luck. On the street, autumn leaves littered the pavement; with her sharp, mincing steps she neither sought nor avoided them. He would hardly have credited that it was her, except you'd know her by the birthmark she has. No way you'd mistake her for somebody else. Dark red, the birthmark: like a wound at the eye.

Beneath the surface of the hot plate, grease has collected. With the back of a spoon, he scrapes it away.

She smiled when he showed her the phone, set more at ease than she had been before. When he'd sat down beside her she had stiffened a bit, clutching her purse instinctively nearer herself. He didn't mind; he wasn't offended. Things are that way in the city. Later, the memory of her initial disquiet will perhaps be something they laugh at together.

He steps back. The kitchenette looks more presentable. In the main room, adjacent, the futon is rumpled, the sheets untidied for several days.

It was chance, good fortune, that brought them together. He will say that if ever they are alone. A blessing for him, and for her as well, because in a strange way they need one another.

He needs her because she might be a friend. He is lonely sometimes, if he's telling the truth. It was the same with the woman he met in the bookshop, but that didn't work out in the end.

She needs him because he alone knows her secret. He has a certain gift for collecting up secrets. In a way, it is a kind of vocation. On Monday he will explain that to her.

He will tell her what he saw those decades ago. He will assure her that all is forgiven.

FROM OLD TELEGRAM Press she makes her way to the bus stop, her coat insufficient to a chill in the air.

She has missed her usual bus, made late because of a misaligned type form. A half run of poetry chapbooks was ruined, or anyway had to have pages replaced. The machine is antique with finicky parts: reglets and quoins that easily loosen, a flywheel that seems to keep an unsteady pace. Angharad ought to have noticed the error—she was supposed to be checking the prints—but some days the girl can hardly be bothered.

"Oh dear, forgive me," Mr. Buchanan said, knowing she dislikes to be kept late. She is paid minimally for her time, the press being run at a perpetual loss, and in exchange its demands of her are minimal, too. He is kind and always has been, Mr. Buchanan. But scattered. These days he is not up to much. At a holiday party, after some wine, he once playfully hinted at marriage. It was an absurd proposition, a joke really, not least because he is gay. "You forget, Robert's only been gone a short time," she said, and he nodded, chastened, being widowed after a fashion himself. Sometimes she wonders how he's got on; thirty years he has managed the press on his own.

At the bus stop she doesn't sit down on the bench, preferring to stand the few minutes alone. There is one other woman waiting with her, disheveled, smacking toothless gums. Normally, she sees the same driver each day. Forrest Clarke, a black man her own age with gray in his beard. He does not ask to see her pass anymore, since they are well acquainted by now. It is a small, simple pleasure at the end of a day. "Darling," he calls her, as if she were young, though he knows she isn't and knows her given name, too. They talk about trivial things from the past: television programs, advertisement jingles. He will have wondered about her today. She will tell him on Monday about lazy Angharad.

When the next bus arrives she pulls herself up the stairs, showing her pass to the unfamiliar driver.

It upsets things, a change in routine. Even a trivial one. You arrange the details of your life, just so, and then something comes along to upend them. She finds a seat near the back and sits down. It makes it harder to manage. She might drive to work—there is still the Capri—but that would bring about its own set of worries. There is comfort in the predictability of her life—the quiet morning commute, the hours she works—as there is comfort in her superficial friendships as well. With Mr. Buchanan, with Forrest. It is routine, not intimacy, she has sought, as it was routine and not love she valued in marriage. Widowed four years, she does not mind the solitude, solitude being her due.

This bus is more crowded than her usual one. Beside her, a boy with a nose ring and headphones taps his foot, keeping time with a song she can't hear. She leans her head back against the rattling window, feels the vibration at the base of her skull.

Perhaps she ought to give up the Capri. It isn't much good to her anymore, averse as she is to the road after dark or if it rains, as it did briefly today. Mr. Buchanan might be able to use it. It has always been well kept and maintained. Even now, it is like new in the garage. Robert believed in that sort of thing.

Lurching, the bus makes a stop and continues; she pulls the cord when her street is announced.

At home, evening has not yet descended. The garden stands awash in westerly light. A rabbit chews at the leaves of a zinnia, but she doesn't chase it away. There is nobody to wheel about a garden anymore, to speak to knowing there will be no response. There was that in youth, Camille in her dresses, and again later, briefly, when Robert was ill.

"Zinnias, Camille," she hears herself saying. "Petunias. Sweet peas. Collard greens. Radish."

Sun falls upon pale, unmoving arms, a face lifted as though to be kissed.

"A rabbit, Camille. Shall we watch him a while?"

She is kind when she thinks of her sister. Gentle. Patient. It is always the same. Today the thoughts have come on a bit early. There is the weekend to negotiate yet.

"WILL YOU DINE with us, or will you take the food in your rooms?"

Mrs. Usak does not bother taking his order because his order is always the same. She wears a blue sweater, large rings on her fingers. Her hair, dyed reddish, is aggressively coifed. To glance at her, one would think she was strong, but he knows how she sometimes suffers at night. He has heard her, after the restaurant closes, lamenting her daughter's licentious behavior. "I should throw her out of the house," she has said, "but I would miss her too much if I did." Since she installed the motion light in the stair-well he has not been able to listen as much, but he watches her, the fatigue in her eyes, the stoop in her shoulders when she walks to the kitchen.

"Here, Mrs. Usak. If it's all the same. I'm off to work soon, as a matter of fact."

In the restaurant now there are two other parties, couples both, seated next to the windows. One, near his own age, eats without speaking. The woman looks sullenly down at her plate. He has chosen a small table facing the room, the better to observe everyone. The other couple is younger, speaking in whispers; they lean forward, disregarding their food.

It is not a good turnout for Saturday lunch. The room appears dark with its wood-paneled walls, its low ceilings, the unoccupied space. They might do well to paint the facade; he has mentioned as much to Mrs. Usak before, feeling entitled since he depends on the place for his room.

The unspeaking woman makes him think of the bookshop. How the wrist, when he touched it, was quickly withdrawn. Nothing was said in that instance, either. Not until later, when she called to complain. Three times in a week he had seen her come in, a thin woman, anxious, with red in her eyes. The books she was buying had to do with conception. He felt for her: a sad thing, the want of a child.

His salad is brought by Mrs. Usak's youngest son. Water is brought, too, silverware, coffee. The waiter's white shirt is buttoned up to the top.

"Anything else for now, sir?" the boy says.

Not looking up, he examines the fork. Last time it had been left a bit scummy. A mistake of that kind will come out of the tip, a savings for him and only fair that it should. Satisfied, he smiles.

"Nothing," he says.

He loved the woman from the bookshop, in fact. For what is love but to suffer another heart's pain? Alone at night, he has thought about her. Two years have passed and he hasn't forgotten. There have been others: sick men who read about death; adolescents who seek comfort in childhood books. To them, he has been forbidden to speak. Arthur has made that perfectly clear.

But the woman from the thirty-six bus is different. With her, there is some chance of connection. What he knows about her is not intuition. He truly is a part of her past. She won't recognize him, but that doesn't matter: she will know when he tells her what it was that he saw. He looks different now, his hair having thinned; years ago, a procedure corrected his vision. Shown a picture, she might say, "Ah yes, I remember. The boy who was always alone." From his stoop or from bus stop benches he watched her. He watched when nobody else was about.

"All right, then?" the waiter says when he returns.

"The seeds of the cucumber might be removed. Of course, I've suggested that in the past. Your mother has her reasons, I'm sure. But it's very good. Timothy, is it? Yes, it's very good, Tim," he says.

The boy stammers something and then moves away, the silent couple having asked for their bill.

The birthmark never spoiled her face. In fact, it lent it a certain distinction. Still it was the sister who was really the beauty, or who would have been. That was often remarked. A certain fineness and resolution in the lines of the face, as if sculpted by a steadier hand.

Those days of his life were spent at loose ends, home for the summer from the school where he lived. At home, as at school, he wasn't paid much attention, a boy, he'd heard it said, of middling promise: not bright in any particular way, not skilled in athletics, not physically strong. Saliva often came thickly to his mouth, a fact he could not help though he tried, and because of that, others disliked eating with him. It spoiled your appetite to see that, they said; Robin Mullins complained to the head of school that it did. His father was hardly ever about, even sleeping some nights in the office. His mother, he had found, required silence at home, her headaches excited by the smallest of sounds. And so, aware, always, of the nuisance he was, he would wander the quiet, unpeopled roads. It was there, while he swung from cherry tree branches, or searched for unusual stones, that he saw them, the one who rides the thirty-six pushing the chair.

Right from the start he fell in love with the sisters. He will tell that to the one on the bus if he can. It wasn't love of the cheap, lurid kind seen in films, nor the childish love he'd heard some claim at school. It was, rather, pure and complete fascination; he loved them the way a person might love the sea. They strolled about, unaware of his gaze, the well sister describing the world for the ill one. The names of things. Their look or their color. Day after day that summer he found them; he walked the roads, searching for them, till he did.

His own bill arrives and he pays it in cash.

"Sister well, Tim?" he says, counting the money. "A nice girl, your sister, I always thought. Tell Mrs. Usak I asked about her. Will you? That I said she was nice?"

IT IS STRANGE that she never dreams of her husband. Waking before dawn, she thinks about that.

He was good: kind in marriage, honest in work. An accountant with a local government office. She ought to make an effort to remember him more. That much he is probably owed.

In the bedroom that they never slept in together, a crack in the curtains reveals the pale sky. The clock on the nightstand reads 5:24, and she turns over knowing sleep won't be reclaimed.

His illness was the happiest time in their lives, weakness drawing her to him as goodness never had. She was grateful in those months for the care he required, grateful because she was busy with him. It had not been an affectionate marriage, a fact that had suited her better than him. In the first, milder months of his illness, he helped her arrange for the sale of their house. He never expressed resentment about that, the ease with which she could cast off the past. "I'd like to be nearer the city," she'd said, and he agreed that that was the sensible thing.

Last night, she dreamed again of Camille: Her pleasure at a flock of geese overhead, at a flower held in front of her face. The way, hearing music, her fingers would move. How she wept, unconsoled, at her grandmother's casket: that woman with hands like the roots of a tree, who'd brought lemon candies and peppermint bark. In the dream, as in life, Camille keened beside her. It hadn't been known whether she understood about death.

Other memories present themselves now. Pretty dresses unworn in the closet; dances, recitals, the leavers ball missed. "Am I to be a nursemaid?" she said, though in fact no invitation had come. "Selfish child," her mother admonished. "It is ugly to envy your sister." Her father said nothing, as ever cowed. He would die young, wounded on behalf of his daughters, not having wanted to outlive the ill one.

Last week she caught her face in a glass. One so seldom looks anymore. There were times when she stared at Camille and cursed the beauty wasted on her.

With her fingers, and by long, unthinking habit, she traces the mark at her eye. Its edges are not discernible to the touch, and yet she knows them exactly by heart.

IN THE BOOKSHOP, customers browse the remainders. A mother reads a picture book to her son.

There are titles to put away, shelves to be tidied. He adjusts the spines so they line up precisely, knowing that Arthur likes them that way. "Try to dress smartly," the head clerk has said. A younger man, Arthur dresses smartly himself. He frowns, regarding the dirt on his own cuffs. It was Arthur, too, who heard the woman's complaint.

Since the incident he has kept a certain distance from customers, speaking only when they ask him for help.

In his school days he always kept a distance as well, trying for friendships tentatively. Seeing the sisters, he had learned to be watchful. He came to know which boys had had letters from home, which had failed an exam or were otherwise troubled. But never did this knowledge lead to a friendship. Sometimes the things he knows about people, the care he has given to observing their lives, makes him feel as if he is brimming with something: a love he has not been allowed to express.

He does not begrudge her any of what he witnessed. That is what he is hoping to say. It can't have been easy, the sister that way. Clearing up after her, pushing the chair. The beautiful sister, the delicate one.

"Filthy," she said the first time he observed it, because the ill sister had vomited. He watched them from the branch of a damson tree, sucking overripe fruit from the seed. When she spoke, he felt at first he'd misheard her, the tenderness falling away from her voice. He'd grown used to a certain measure of violence: teachers or students speaking harshly at school, his own mother losing patience with him. Only that morning his parents had fought; yet, somehow, he wasn't prepared for this cruelty: The quiet. The intimacy.

The well sister knelt down in front of the ill one, cleaning the liquid with a napkin she held. "What a foul, wretched creature," she said. Lips firmly abraded, an ear roughly pulled.

It was hot out and he felt the sweat pricking his neck. Tears in his eyes caused his glasses to fog. As they carried on, away down the road, he felt the great burdensome weight of his body.

"A millstone," she said on other occasions, while the ill sister quietly wept. Flesh was many times prodded or pinched; firm blows were applied to the ribs.

At the front desk, he refills the register tape. He offers to place a man's book in a bag.

"Plans for your weekend?" Arthur says, meaning Monday and Tuesday because he is off.

When that summer ended he returned to his school, but memories of the sisters remained. He carried them in his heart through the winter; on Sundays in chapel his prayers were for them. He wasn't surprised when news came of his parents' divorce. His first thought was not of his mother or father, those distant figures he had not come to know. It was, rather, about the two sisters he'd watched and whether he would ever see them again.

"Yes," he tells Arthur, "as a matter of fact. Monday I am going to see an old friend."

THE BUS SIGHS as it pulls away from her stop, and she takes her seat in the usual place. She slept poorly last night, as all weekend she did, agitation remaining despite her fatigue. It is still there now, though the morning has soothed it, this resumption of her weekly routine.

On Afton, they stop at Meadowlark and then Charles. An ad above a window says It's Never Too Late. At Bradbury, she looks to the front, aware vaguely of somebody's gaze. A man pays his fare, stealing glances at her; she suppresses an urge to lift a hand to her face. He wears a blue slicker over his shirt, a pale one with a collar, a tie loosely done. Six feet or so and average in other respects: balding in the usual way, his skin pale and pitted from childhood acne. She has seen him before, last week on the bus. In any other context she wouldn't remember, but here, in this space, the memory rises. The rain he predicted for Friday has come; he smiles a little as he approaches, lifts his eyes as if to acknowledge the fact. Even then there was something about him. When he leaned in to show her his cellular phone, his fingernails were long and unclean.

Her umbrella has been folded and placed on the seat beside her, so he sits down in the one next to that. At once, he can feel her recoil, the almost imperceptible movement away. He does not take offense, as he didn't on Friday. Soon he will speak and she will see he is kind. He has tried to dress smartly today.

The birthmark is on the left side of her face, the one that is nearest to him. The red of it is carnal and deep, as if a piece of her heart were on the outside. She is beautiful, more so than in youth. Lines have been etched about her mouth and her eyes, but in other ways she is unchanged, her face still recalling the ill sister's, too.

Aware of his shifting eyes, she is nervous. There is something prying in the way he regards her. She looks around the near-empty bus, a pretense sought for moving away.

At the next stop, more riders board. Their presence is a comfort to her.

"If only that were true," he says, lifting an arm. It is the ad he refers to—It's Never Too Late—and at once she is made nervous again.

She smiles weakly, not meeting his eye, then stands and moves herself nearer the door.

"Miss," he says. "Madame."

Other riders look up.

"Your umbrella. You mustn't forget that today." His arm is outstretched, holding the thing.

When pain was inflicted upon the ill sister she turned aside, as if ashamed to be seen. Your heart wanted to break when you saw her. You never loved a creature more in the world. But it wanted to break for the well sister, too, who would slump a little, fatigued by remorse, and resume with the chair, more gingerly now.

At length, she accepts the umbrella, taking care that their hands shouldn't touch.

She waits until the last moment to pull the cord for her stop, stepping down without calling thanks to the driver.

On the street, the rain has slowed to a drizzle. The sidewalks appear darkened and slick. She moves quickly, is nearing the press when she hears him, a thin voice calling her name.

"Rose, is it?"

She turns. "Now what's this about?"

Some people have paused to observe. A man with a paper cup for loose change stands and moves a short way down the block.

"It's Myron," he says. "Myron Idris. The boy who was always alone."

He regards her face, not looking away, no longer surreptitious or shy. He tries to discern friendship, recognition. He beseeches her for it, thinking that word.

Beseeching.

"I used to watch you. Pushing your sister."

Rigidly, she stands without speaking. One finger strokes the leather strap of her purse, the gesture repeated like a kind of devotion. She says, "I don't know what you're talking about."

"I watched you all through the summer. In Glass. I loved you. Both you and your sister I loved."

A wind rises, stirring up leaves from the ground. A blue plastic shopping bag scrapes past his feet.

Vaguely, she sees the outline of an image: a boy with eyeglasses, a twig in his hand.

"I've often felt my whole life began when I saw you."

Her face, which for the briefest moment had softened, now quickly hardens again. In her eyes is the same look he saw in the bookshop when the touch of his hand caused a woman's revulsion. He goes on, a little desperately now: "Imagine it, after so many years, and in the city: That we should meet in this way."

An old gentleman steps out of the press. He stands in the doorway, holding a broom.

"I could hardly believe it when I saw you last week. 'It can't be,' I said, but I knew that it was."

"I don't know who you are," she says. "Stop it. Please."

"Is there a problem?" the old man is saying. "Mrs. Goodrum, is this man bothering you?"

"I saw everything. You are not to be blamed. That's all I ever wanted to say."

In her heart is a pain she can scarcely withstand, an uncanny mix of gratitude and disgust. She feels she would fall to her knees if she could, or that she would run, that she would do herself harm. What she did to Camille has been her secret alone, a shame that made up the better part of herself. She hadn't known that she'd wanted to share it, that she'd longed for someone to say what he has. She has not wished for love, but he offers it, regardless: this madman, this lunatic does.

"I loved you more because your strength broke," he says. "It was cruel, but cruelty is part of us, too."

She nods, meeting his eye for a moment, then turns away toward the old man's embrace. She moves without any violence or speed, but he can see nonetheless that the gesture is final. She would not wish to meet him in a café for tea or to dine at Usak's near the window with him. He knows that, as he should have before. Never would she wish to visit his rooms. If he cleaned them, if he dressed more smartly, she still wouldn't. If he rides her bus again she will call the police; if, by chance, he encounters her again in the city she will cross to the other side of the street.

"It's all right, Rose," he says, calling after her faintly.

Passing through the door of the office, she hears it.

"I know everything," he says. "It's all right."

In fact, he knows very little at all. He does not know, for instance, what became of Camille, how she screamed when they left her behind in the home, how one day she seemed to cease wishing to live. He does not know about the sound she made while she slept, a wet, guttural clicking at the back of the throat. How it woke the well sister in the dark of the night, a sound as familiar as crickets or rain. He does not know that the sound was thought to signal a dream, of what exactly no one could know. A dream of running, perhaps. Of being led in a waltz. Of singing. Of saying, "You're hurting me, love."

On those nights, the well sister would rise, apply a compress until the clicking had ceased. She would reach down and touch the beautiful face with the rag—a face that, in sleep, was as though unafflicted—and kiss the cool dampness left behind on the skin. He does not know that. Nobody does. How in the quiet that followed she imagined a violence, the same one she sometimes imagines today. It is a great violence, absolute and pristine, like the one that long ago created the world.

ACKNOWLEDGMENTS

✕ ✕ ✕

A FIRST BOOK is a delicate thing. (So, at times, is its author.) Thank you to my agent, Janet Silver, for so fiercely protecting this one. Thank you to my editor, Kathy Pories, Brunson Hoole, Michael McKenzie, Lauren Moseley, Craig Popelars, and the rest of the team at Algonquin, for giving it shelter.

Thank you to those editors who took an early chance: Brigid Hughes; Wendy Lesser; Sudip Bose. And to those institutions who supported the work: University of California, Davis; the University of Iowa. Thanks to Vincent Torre and the Museo Giardino Irene Brin in Sasso di Bordighera, Italy.

I am grateful for the generosity of my many fine teachers, each of whom answered that highest of callings. From Berkeley Unified: Ann Gilbert. From UC Davis: Jodi Angel, Clarence Major, Pam Houston, Lucy Corin, Lynn Freed. From the Iowa Writers' Workshop: Lan Samantha Chang, Kevin Brockmeier, Marilynne Robinson, Paul Harding, Ethan Canin, Margot Livesey. Elsewhere: Ron Carlson, Jess Walter.

Thanks to my classmates at UC Davis for friendship and faith, and for those many late nights at Danny's apartment: Ashley Clarke, Megan Cummins, Daniel Grace, Maria Kuznetsova, Noah McGee, Carrie Newman, Richard Siegler. Let this be the first book of many for us.

The opportunity to spend three years at the Iowa Writers' Workshop was among the great privileges of my life. Many thanks to Deb West and Jan Zenisek. Thank you, again and forever, Sam Chang.

Connie Brothers is a national treasure. Thank you, Connie.

My workshop classmates read these stories with tremendous care and attention. My deepest gratitude to Garth Greenwell, for advocacy, insight, and the highest example; Fatima Farheen Mirza, who reads, as she writes, with her whole heart; Chia-Chia Lin, who is, quite simply, a genius, and whose reading gave a breath of new life to this book; and Jamel Brinkley, who was my first, best friend in that strange place, and whom I admire immensely.

Thanks also to Noel Carver, Jed Cohen, Heidi Kaloustian, Nyuol Lueth Tong, and the many others, too numerous to name, whose talent, sincerity, and relentless exactitude have imprinted themselves on this project.

I fear I can never adequately thank Yiyun Li—teacher, mentor, friend—who believed in these stories long before I did, and without whose seemingly bottomless generosity and wisdom this book would not exist, in any form.

Thank you to my family for their love and support. My parents, Julie and Geoffrey. My sister, Emily. Kevin. Ann. David. Elliot. In memory of Bill and Nell Owen, of Frank and Lee Tarloff.

And to my partner, Ellen Namakaokealoha Kamoe, who is so deeply good, and so kind, who hears even what is said in a whisper.